D1098353

Julie Bertagna was born in Ayrshire and grew up near Glasgow. After an English degree at Glasgow University, she worked as the editor of a small magazine, as a teacher and then as a freelance journalist for various publications.

She was awarded the Scottish Arts Council Bursary after the publication of *The Spark Gap*, her first novel. *Soundtrack* won the Scottish Arts Council's Children's Book Award and was selected for the Library Association's Scottish Writers' Project in secondary schools. *Dolphin Boy* was shortlisted for the NASEN Award and the Blue Peter Book Awards. Her first novel for Macmillan, *Exodus*, was shortlisted for the Whitbread Award and was described by the *Guardian* as 'a miracle of a novel'. It won the Lancashire Book Award. Her *The Ice-cream Machine* books for younger children have been developed for television.

Julie writes full-time and lives in Glasgow with her family.

Julie Bertagna

the spark gap

YOUNG PICADOR

For their belief and support, my heartfelt thanks to the late Herta Ryder, Jean Morris and my long-distance soul-mate, Steve Davis

First published 1996 by Egmont Children's Books Limited

This edition published 2005 by Young Picador
an imprint of Pan Macmillan Limited
20 New Wharf Road, London N1 9RR
Basingstoke and Oxford
www.panmacmillan.com

Associated companies throughout the world

ISBN 0 330 41812 2

Copyright © Julie Bertagna 1996

The right of Julie Bertagna to be identified as the
author of this work has been asserted by her in accordance
with the Copyright, Designs and Patents Act 1988.

All rights reserved. No part of this publication may be
reproduced, stored in or introduced into a retrieval system, or
transmitted, in any form, or by any means (electronic, mechanical,
photocopying, recording or otherwise) without the prior written
permission of the publisher. Any person who does any unauthorized
act in relation to this publication may be liable to criminal
prosecution and civil claims for damages.

1 3 5 7 9 8 6 4 2

A CIP catalogue record for this book is available from
the British Library.

Typeset by Intype Libra Ltd
Printed and bound in Great Britain by Mackays of Chatham plc, Kent

This book is sold subject to the condition that it shall not,
by way of trade or otherwise, be lent, re-sold, hired out,
or otherwise circulated without the publisher's prior consent
in any form of binding or cover other than that in which
it is published and without a similar condition including this
condition being imposed on the subsequent purchaser.

For Riccardo

MORAY COUNCIL LIBRARIES & INFO.SERVICES	
2O 15 34 57	
Askews	
JCY	

Contents

Part one: Gran and the gang

Part two: The roof

Part three: Finding Avalon

Part one
Gran and the gang

The storm takes Gran

Great drops of rain burst in the shape of fried eggs and streamed messily down the tall windows that ran the length of the school gym hall.

Kerrie sat on a pile of spongy gym mats, thinking what an unwatery sound it was as the rain crescendoed to full battering pitch. The outbreak of bad temper around her had calmed for a moment, fizzled out like a squib of drenched firework. But already they were off again.

'It was you. You were away all over the place.'

'I only lost it 'cause you did.'

'It was all out. Out of time, out of key, out, out . . .'

'Aah, I'm packing it in.'

Sarah crashed the keyboards and the hall filled with the sound of disgust. In retaliation, Shell exploded on to the drumkit and became a fury, a mass of thrashing hair that tangled in her sticks. Janis swallowed a sigh, unplugged her microphone, and began to unravel its tangled length of flex.

Kerrie watched the rain patterns on the windows and

wound a strand of hair tight, tight round a finger till the tip turned purple. She curled up her toes till they cramped and rolled her tongue between her teeth. Stupid, she told herself. Shell and Sarah were just scrapping. They were always scrapping about something; they enjoyed it, really, even if she didn't. The best thing to do was just stand back, give them plenty of space, and eventually they'd battle themselves into boredom.

Shell and Sarah enjoyed being at cross purposes. Kerrie remembered her first day at secondary school when, stomach queasy with nerves, she'd been put at the table for those with surnames beginning 'Mc'. She had sat swapping shy glances with Janis, while Shell and Sarah squabbled over the ownership of a pencil topped with a green plastic troll. At breaktime, the four of them had huddled in a corner of the playground, feeling like twitchy minnows in a terrifyingly big pool. From that day they had been a foursome, meeting after school to discuss every twist and turn of their thoughts. On a long, grey stretch of last summer's school holiday, when it bucketed down every single day. Shell had had one of her brainwaves and their band, the Restless Souls, was born.

The sight of Shell brandishing her drumsticks high in the air, right above Sarah's head, broke through Kerrie's thoughts. Sarah had snatched up Janis's bass guitar and was sunk in an irritating bass riff. The bass throbbed like a headache, and Shell growled, a peculiar warning technique that she had developed from living in a house full of cats and interfering infants.

Kerrie uncurled. Time to break it up.

It always happened like this, she thought. Just when the music got good, seemed to catch the sound of itself and freewheel off on an interesting whim of its own, the band got grumpy. One by one they broke under the strain and disintegrated into silence or squabbling.

We just can't cope with being good, Kerrie decided, rubbing the tingling tip of her pinkie as it revived from the temporary halt in its blood supply.

A bad habit, that. At least the toe and tongue curling didn't upset her guitar playing. Neither did they upset Gran, who could spot most things but not a secretly scrunched toe. It was the last remaining habit from a string of fidgets. Gran had provided Kerrie with calm and steady love, and a whole range of undermining tactics to get rid of the fidgets: cuddles that left you with a mouthful of mohair cardigan and a sweet in your hand; special midnight cups of tea with the biscuit box and a good gossip. But nothing had, as yet, beaten the curliewurlie habit.

Kerrie took up her guitar and polished away a fingerprint with her sleeve. Gran surely couldn't have afforded it. A brand-new top-of-the-range model, an acoustic that you could also plug in and play electric. The sound of it was honey on hot, soft bread.

The guitar was the first thing Kerrie saw when she opened her eyes each morning. Every day, she thrilled at the sight. Before she got into bed at night she would polish off the day's accumulation of fingerprints with a soft cloth, and prop the guitar against the wall so that it faced her. She would fall asleep imagining up some new song in her head.

Now she sat with the guitar flat across her knees, feeling the strings with the very tips of her fingers, as they buzzed and vibrated with the force of the storm outside. The rain seemed to have battered all the energy out of the other three now. They were in danger of leaving yet another Saturday practice in a huff, and it usually took until Monday for the snarling to stop.

Kerrie turned up her amplifier, and watched a streaming window. She tuned into the water patterns and let her fingers follow them until gradually she found a dripping run of blues.

Sarah, sprawled under the keyboards feigning sleep, grinned. She resisted just until she heard Shell give in and break into a pattering drumbeat. Then suddenly the hall was full of wandering keyboards, as Sarah kicked off her mood like a pair of old trainers and the various parts of the music began to knit.

Already packed up, jacketed, and ready to go, Janis cast her eyes to the ceiling and sat down on the dusty floor. In an instant she was on her feet again making cut-throat gestures as the janitor appeared through a swing door, with a face like a prune, as Shell would say. The storm of sound cut dead as quick as if the jannie had snipped a power cable. A corridor of fire doors swung in his wake, as if battered by a class of invisible year nines.

'I should think so.'

He gave each word the weight of a full second. 'A right midden of a noise, that. Time you were all away home getting the tea on for your mothers instead of organizing a racket like that.'

The jannie snapped the shiny steel jaws of his litter-clipper, subduing the Restless Souls into a scuttling, heads-down silence. He followed them all the way down the corridor, his litter-clipper snapping like a sheepdog desperate to nip at their heels.

'What's he like?' muttered Shell. '"Tea for your mothers." Does he say that to the five-a-sides? Does he heck.'

She kept up her anti-jannie monologue until they turned the corner at the end of the school block, where they were almost blown flat by the gust of rain that hit them.

'My da says it's just a big wind tunnel, this,' yelled Janis, as the four of them linked arms against the blast from the gap between the buildings that stretched the length of the hill.

Halfway down the hill the puddle-grey exteriors of the terraced houses became candyfloss pink and custard yellow. The housing-renovation programme had run out of money between numbers ten and eleven, sparking a feud between the painted and unpainted residents of Strawberryhill Road.

Everything had been built the wrong way round, too. The two-storey terraces should really have been situated on the hill instead of the cluster of giant tower blocks which stood rooted at the top, a menace in their hugeness, overlooking Glasgow like a band of sentinels. Kerrie had her usual split-second, edge-of-thought shudder at the sight of the louring buildings.

'I tell you though,' Sarah yelled over the wind as they separated into pairs at the roundabout, 'that last bit was something. Too good. The Restless Souls'll tour the world yet,' Sarah grinned and ran across the road to the street she and Janis lived in, punching out a clenched salute.

'Tomorrow the world then,' smiled Janis, following Sarah at her usual infuriatingly steady pace.

Kerrie and Shell were heads down against the wind as they took the road up the hill to their tower block. With a guilty pang Kerrie pictured Gran, thirty floors up, struggling alone with the storm shoogle, as she called it. On days such as this, everything that was able to rattled and shifted, unless it slammed or clattered, in the sway of the wind. Gran said it shoogled you worse than a ride on the old trams.

Doors, mirrors, lamps and ornaments, all the loose bits and pieces of the bathroom and the kitchen, they all became uncontrollable. Kerrie could close her eyes on wild days and imagine herself on some futuristic train, hurtling through the sky.

Shell gave a loud scream right in Kerrie's ear. A large cardboard box plastered with wet litter was bouncing down the hill straight towards them. Then Shell got crazy and danced with it in the middle of the road. The box tired of her game and bounded off in a new direction, luring a small band of dogs that had been hanging around the bus stop. As the box switched direction again and hurled itself into the face of an oncoming bus, the two girls shrieked, expecting the dogs to follow. The bus shuddered to a standstill but the dogs were already off again on another chase.

'Now you'd never get a cat being that daft,' giggled Shell, who knew all there was to know about cats. Her flat was something of a cat sanctuary due to the ever-changing selection of strays found on the stairways by her father. His habit of championing the weak and the dispossessed, after a bout of losing on the horses, made him feel he wasn't quite the lowest of the low after he'd blown half the week's housekeeping, Shell reasoned.

They hurried as they approached a huddle of youths at the great squat feet of the tower block. Shell checked out the state of the lifts, wrinkled up her face and chose the least offensive.

'Come on up to mine,' said Kerrie, as she did every Saturday. 'It's pizza.'

'Spicy sausage,' said Shell hopefully, well aware that Kerrie's gran knew her preferences. 'I'll hug her to death if it's a spicy sausage one.'

They always got a thorough spoiling by Gran, whereas at Shell's it was a case of elbowing for space among cats and nappies and assorted family members. The McCormacks were a large family who lived at top volume. Kerrie would come home to the calm of Gran cooking dinner and humming along to the radio, and her ears would be ringing.

The lift lurched up thirty floors.

'Oh no, forgot the milk.' Kerrie opened the front door. 'Gran, I've done it again.'

Margaret, their next-door neighbour, appeared in the kitchen doorway.

'Oh, hen,' she whispered.

'What?' Kerrie was irritated, as always, by Margaret and her hovering. She wished Gran would stop encouraging her 'five-minute' visits. Especially on Saturdays. It meant that they would have to do without being waited on hand and foot, Gran making funny, dry comments as she was bombarded with the latest details of the Restless Souls' bid for stardom.

'Oh, hen.'

Margaret was repeating herself as usual. She rubbed her hands together as if she was cold. Her face looked odd. The silly, pink, doll cheeks were stretched and pale.

Kerrie felt something slide sickeningly in her stomach as a figure with a briefcase came out of Gran's room.

Behind Margaret, the kitchen was empty.

'Doctor'll tell you,' whispered Margaret, looking guilty.

Shell's grip on Kerrie's arm tightened as the doctor cleared his throat. He was telling her something awful, Kerrie knew, yet the words jumbled and made no sense. Shell gave a gasp and began to back away. 'I'll get my mum,' she was saying, and then she was gone.

Kerrie stumbled into Gran's bedroom, feeling as if

she were falling down an endless dark lift shaft, falling in the dark left behind by the awful thing that had burst in with the storm while she was out, and had whisked Gran away.

Kerrie lay on her bed listening to the wind fling itself against the side of the tower block with the force of a tidal wave. The tall building grappled with each burst, sending her collection of ceramic frogs, the happy face alarm clock and a mug of scummy tea off on a shuffling march across the surface of the dressing table.

On any other day the frog race would've set her giggling, she would've had Gran in for a bet on who'd take a nosedive first off the edge of the dressing table.

The mug of tea looked disgusting. It had been sitting there for hours. Margaret had tiptoed in with it, her fat cheeks deflated and twitching like punctured balloons. The mug was right on target for a maths ink exercise. It lay on the floor half-done and due in to Mrs Buchanan first thing Monday morning, no excuses allowed except sudden death. Your own. Nobody else's, not even your favourite granny's.

Kerrie shut her eyes.

She had tried not to think about it. She had tried not to think at all but it kept coming back to her: at break-fast Gran had seemed odd. Her face had that tight look about it that the angina pains sometimes brought on. Gran's chest pains came and went, yet she insisted they were nothing to worry about. Even though they stopped her doing anything in a hurry, trapped her thirty floors off the ground for days on end whenever the lifts weren't working. But as soon as Gran had caught Kerrie watching her she'd joked about giving up the karate, that would likely be the cause of it. Then she'd furrowed her fingers in her short, unfussed hair – a bothered gesture that Kerrie should have taken heed of. It was unexpected in someone Gran's age, Kerrie always thought. You wouldn't get Margaret running her fingers through her rollered and laquered hair – they'd get stuck halfway in a tangle of solid, wiry curls.

But, like her habit of never eating the crusts of her bread and always having a fusty toffee and a rustle of sweet papers in the corner of her pockets, Gran had held on to the silly, quirky ways you were supposed to grow out of once you became a sensible adult. It was her small rebellion against old age. And she never did the little-old-lady act. So Kerrie had taken Gran at her word, gulped down her tea and toast, and rushed out to the band's Saturday morning practice.

The mug of cold tea shuddered towards the edge of the dressing table. Kerrie watched it hesitate, then topple and land on her maths jotter as the thought pulsed and pulsed until it made a headache. If she had paid more attention, if she hadn't been so self-centred and gone out this morning, she could have called the doctor right away.

Then Gran might not have died.

*

12

Something shrill sounded in the silent flat. Kerrie shook herself free of a damp tangle of quilt, her head still fuzzy with sleep, and listened.

Only the phone, silly.

She sat up and saw eyes staring back at her from the dressing-table mirror, eyes that were so tight and raw they didn't look like her own. The phone continued to shriek.

Margaret had told her what to say if anyone called while she ran down to the shops. A supply of tea and plain biscuits, Margaret had decided, was the key to their survival over the next couple of days.

Mum had arrived. She was not to be disturbed, though it was unlikely she would budge now if you set off a firework right next to her. She had been found at the number Gran had pinned up on the Don't Forget board in the kitchen – surprisingly, since Mum's phone numbers often had strict use-by dates. She'd sat stoppering her mouth with her knuckles, sobs in her throat like water in a clogged drain, only unplugging for gulps of whisky, and was now a liquescent heap on the living-room couch.

Margaret had only shaken her head and whispered into the carpet as she cleared up the debris that always sprang up, like a patch of blue mould, around Mum's feet. In bursting plastic bags, Mum carried around such life essentials as stretchy cycling shorts, her horoscope book and an album crammed with unstuck photos.

Kerrie walked down the hall and took the phone off

the hook, ignoring the voice at the other end as she stuffed the receiver in one of Gran's sheepskin slippers which were neatly parked under the phone seat. In the living room, Mum was still spread all over the couch, snoring unevenly. Kerrie felt a giggle in her throat at the thought of the rollicking Gran would have given Mum if she'd caught her in a state like that.

Then, crumpled and blurry-faced, Mum suddenly woke and Kerrie found herself staring into cat-green eyes that were so like her own. Sitting on the arm of Gran's chair, Kerrie felt an old emotion tear at her. She couldn't have given the emotion a name. It was anger and pity and something else painful, all mixed up. On top of the awfulness of Gran's death it was just too much.

'Kerrie,' Mum was calling as she left the room. 'Wait now. Kerrie, I know.'

Do you hell, Kerrie thought, locking the bathroom door behind her and turning on the hot bath tap full pelt.

Margaret's grey perm had sprung to a violent frizz in the rain. Whispering away to herself, she filled Gran's large red teapot with boiling water. Margaret was always praying about something. She kept a list in her handbag of things and people needing a pray.

Well, now she had good reason, thought Kerrie.

In the heat of the kitchen Margaret's angular spectacle lenses began to mist and her cheeks plumped up like cushions.

Kerrie fought back the urge to slap one of Margaret's silly red cheeks and decided she'd better get out before she did something awful.

As Kerrie took her jacket from the back of a kitchen chair, Margaret looked as if a sudden pain had gripped her somewhere.

'Oh, but where are you going, hen? What about your mum? Just go in and see how she's feeling. You should be sticking together at a time like this, taking care of each other.'

Kerrie felt something nip at her, guilt or anger, and turned on Margaret.

'Take care of that disaster? Stick with her? That'll be right.'

Margaret seemed to decide Kerrie was upset or just being a teenage brat. But Gran was no hypocrite. Surely she'd told Margaret about Mum.

'Well, you two will just have to get sorted out,' Margaret was murmuring now. 'I mean, now that your gran's . . . not with us any more you'll have to go back to your mum. So let's start the way we mean to go on. That's the best, isn't it?'

As Kerrie kicked a table leg for getting in her way, she saw with a shock that Margaret was right enough. There was no longer a home for her here. And there was no one else, apart from Mum. She'd have to . . . Kerrie cut the thought. She would not go back to Mum.

'I'm away out,' Kerrie said, her voice sullen, unlike itself.

She pushed past Margaret and her teapot and ran blindly out through the front door, along the corridor to the lifts.

Homeless

Shell splashed out four mugs of loud, green limeade. She was trying desperately, flamboyantly, to act as if tonight was any other Saturday night. Now she'd started a frantic drumbeat with two pens on the rim of her mug. Shell knew it wasn't working.

'Grab,' she commanded. 'Oh, and I've got vodka if anyone fancies some,' she added, deliberately casual. 'Under the bed.'

A scramble under the bed, less casual, ensued.

'Where'd you get that then?' asked Janis.

Shell played inscrutable.

'Och, there's hardly a splash there,' said Janis and poured out four minute measures.

'How ungrateful,' Shell tutted, flinging crisp packets wildly. 'Catch.'

'Your da'll go mental again, left with the Deadly Salted,' said Janis.

Shell forced a loud laugh, and frowned hard at Sarah who was ignoring everything, even the packet of crisps that had landed beside her.

After a minute of rapid gulping and crunching, Janis licked the salt grains off her fingers and wiped her hands on the bedspread. She picked up a notebook and pen and stared at Shell.

'The – um – problem is . . .' began Shell.

Janis printed the word PROBLEM in huge capitals at the top of her page.

In the opposite corner Sarah lolled on Shell's tartan beanbag, peeling off the corner of a poster, sunk in herself as usual. Kerrie always sensed that a great part of Sarah was cut off from the rest of them; there was a dark loneliness about her. Shell just thought she was a moody, wee toerag.

'But they're the only ones who could get her a house,' Kerrie heard Janis say. 'If they thought she'd a good enough reason.'

'Well she has,' Shell argued. 'Her mum's no' fit to look after her . . .' She tailed off and scrabbled up her long curls till they were as wild as her mint-blue eyes.

'Maybe if we told them what your mum was like,' Shell said, 'Then they'd have to do something for you. That's what they're supposed to be there for.'

Kerrie began to scrape the label off the limeade bottle with her thumbnail. She shook her head. Despite everything, she couldn't betray Mum like that to outsiders, to someone official like social workers. The thought turned her stomach. Gran would never have understood her doing a thing like that either because no matter what, Gran's door had always been open to

Mum. 'A daughter's a daughter,' she'd say, and grimace at Kerrie. Even when that daughter's your daft, mixed-up mother. And a mother's a mother, Kerrie supposed, no matter how unmotherly she actually was.

Shell, who had been watching her closely, leaned over and gave Kerrie a hug.

'I suppose I couldny tell if it was my mum. I could maybe tell on that Sharon though for the terrible cruelty she inflicts on me. I mean look at the state she's left that dressing table in. It's torture sharing a bedroom with her.' Shell's older sister was heavily into make-up and clothes, and always left a trail of each in her wake.

'If you told the Social Work they'd do something all right,' said Sarah, her voice even more raw than usual. She appeared to find something fascinating on the strip of paper she'd just torn off the poster.

Shell restrained her annoyance at this vandalism of her property. On hearing about Kerrie's gran, Sarah had retreated into one of her fiercest silences and any niggle could cause her to withdraw back into herself. But they needed Sarah just now. She knew all about social workers.

'What would they do?' asked Kerrie.

'They'd put you in a nice new home,' said Sarah. 'Like they did with us when my da was in prison and my ma went loopy. A children's home or a foster home.'

There was a stunned silence.

'I don't want that,' said Kerrie. 'Strangers.'

19

'Well, we won't go near Them then,' said Shell. 'Now . . .'

'Look,' said Sarah, 'are you guys serious or are we just playing games to make Kerrie feel better?' She looked stonily from Janis to Shell.

'We . . .' Shell started, then stopped, and began a drum-roll on her mug.

'It's serious,' said Kerrie at last. 'I'm no' going back to her and her crazy life. Never.'

'OK, Sarah, spill it. *Please*,' said Janis.

Sarah needed to be cajoled into most things even if it was something she was desperate to do. She just could not be seen to look enthusiastic about anything.

Sarah took time to rearrange her long legs on the beanbag. Her pale, sulky face relaxed. Sarah's version of a smile.

'I know where you can go,' she said to Kerrie.

Kerrie's stomach heaved. Knowing Sarah, she was unsure if she wanted to hear.

'The roof,' said Sarah. 'The rooftop of these flats.'

A great sigh swept round the room.

'Och, Sarah.'

'You big doughball.'

'It's perfect,' said Sarah calmly. 'Any of you ever been up there?'

'You canny get up there, thicko. There's locks and caretakers and everything,' said Shell. 'And if you can get up there'll be junkies there.'

'Nope,' said Sarah. 'There's no been a caretaker for years and the keys that fit the midgies fit the roof as

20

well. See, there used to be laundry rooms up there. They're never used now.'

The midgies were the sheds at the base of the flat where the rubbish bins were kept. Their name came from the insect clouds that engulfed them in the summer.

'And how could Kerrie live on a rooftop?' Janis asked scathingly.

'People do,' said Sarah, reaching at last for her bag of crisps.

'What people?' asked Shell.

'Dopeheads,' laughed Janis. 'Don't start dreaming, Shell. That's great, Sarah. Kerrie can go and live in a junkie den.'

'They're no' junkies,' said Sarah. 'I've met them. I went a wander one night after I left here. Things were a bit crazy at home and I wanted some peace. I ended up on the roof. They shooed me off but next time I took them up a bundle of sweeties and they were OK.'

'So who are they?' asked Kerrie, after a pause. She needed to fasten on to something other than the nightmare.

'Just a guy and a girl. Skip's homeless so he lives up there. Mauve, she paints.'

'Paints?' Shell creased up her face. Sarah could have said skydives. 'Why?'

'Because she's a painter, dumbo. Her pictures are brilliant.'

Everyone stared at Sarah. She flushed red but stared them out.

21

'Mauve. Nice name, that,' said Shell.

'What does she paint?' asked Kerrie.

Sarah waved an arm in a wide arc in front of her.

'Wild things. The city and the sky and these strange people. And *huge* patterns all over the roof. Real spacey stuff.'

Sarah suddenly dried up and sank back into the beanbag.

'But when it rains,' said Shell, 'all her pictures'll get washed away.'

'So she does new ones. She don't care. She says they're only for the moment they're done. She does lots more on paper anyway.'

'Oh,' said Shell.

'Never mind her pictures. Where do *they* go when it rains?' asked Janis. 'Where do they sleep, eat, get washed, get money for food, et cetera, et cetera?'

Janis had ended up looking stupid once too often.

Sarah shrugged. 'They manage.' She turned to Kerrie. 'I'm telling you, It's perfect.' Sarah's face creased into what was very nearly a grin.

Glances were exchanged around the room.

Kerrie shrugged. Her mind had gone blank, she couldn't seem to think what it was they were asking of her. And she was unnerved by the thing that was pressing in at the window, carrying into the room on grains of the dark. A black heaving thing, growing out of the shadows in the corners of the room. She didn't want to think about it. But something had been decided anyway.

'We can always beat her up,' said Shell, baring her teeth at Sarah and hitting an imaginary cymbal, 'if she's telling a load of porky pies. Let's check this out.'

Mauve paints an emerald sunset

It was like stepping out on to another world.

The dusk was gathering gritty particles of darkness, bringing on the night. But now that she was out among them, Kerrie saw that the grains of dark hung separate and calm as stars; no great louring beast was drawing itself up, swarming thickly out of the night, after all.

Bleak shapes littered the rooftop: oil-drums, crates, piles of tarpaulin. And a sound, wailing and unworldly, carried on the air. A sound almost like music. It came from the far side of the roof, from behind one of the two block-shaped sheds. The wailing music rose eerily, wavered and fell into a long, low note. Then faded.

'What is it?' whispered Shell, squeaking on the 'it'. Her eyes were wide and pale in the heavy light.

'Just Skip,' Sarah whispered back.

'But what *is* it?' Janis sounded frantic too.

'A mouth organ, stupid,' said Sarah, walking towards the sound.

Of course, thought Kerrie, I remember. Grandpa used to play one.

'Come on.'

They followed Sarah, who was already halfway across the coloured patterns that covered the roof floor. Kerrie stooped down and touched part of it. A dry dust stained her fingertips.

Chalk.

There were more patterns on the shed walls. In the fading light they were only vague impressions, but Kerrie imagined them wild and brilliant in daylight.

'Look,' said Sarah from the edge of the roof.

Beyond the mesh fence that enclosed the rooftop were lights, thousands upon thousands of them. Overhead, the sky had blown clear of the day's storm into a starry image of the city below.

Kerrie pressed her face and her body aganst the cold wire of the fence and stretched her arms above her head, hooking her fingers through the mesh holes. A soft, cool wind touched her face.

Look at it all. Don't think. Just look.

She released herself from the fence. Shell was giggling at her.

'You've got criss-cross lines all over your face now, diddy. Come on. We've to meet Mauve.'

Shell pulled her to where the others stood. Kerrie looked over Janis's shoulder at a small figure sitting on a wooden crate. Sarah was kneeling down, murmuring to Mauve as she worked deep colours on to a large canvas that was attached to the mesh fence. The light of a torch focused on the painting. Occasionally Mauve nodded but she never stopped.

'Magic, eh?' said Shell, her eyes fixed on the painting.

Then Mauve spoke abruptly. 'Can't stop, I need to catch those last dregs of colour over there.' She nodded towards the long, low streaks of sunset.

Kerrie studied what she could see of Mauve, which wasn't too much, side-on in the near darkness. The most striking thing was her overload of jewellery: it covered her like a web of wet seaweed, glinting slimily in the cavernous dusk. On the ear that Kerrie could see there were four or five different earrings. A small jewel stud glinted at the side of her nose. She wore brightly patterned bangles high on her arm over a dark top, and brooches were pinned to the front of it among a tangle of necklaces. Only her hands were free. Her dark hair was cropped short except for a few long wispy strands around her face. She had a fierce set to her face and looked about seventeen, Kerrie decided, comparing her to some of the older girls at school.

A noise distracted her and Kerrie looked over her shoulder. Crouched and half-hidden behind one of the sheds was a boy. But as soon as Kerrie glimpsed him the boy pulled back out of sight.

'Damn,' said Mauve. 'I'm never quick enough.'

The sliver of orange sun had suddenly slipped behind the black shadow of the city.

'All the colours'll change now. See.'

Already the edges of the sunset were melting into dark smoke, blue-green and yellow. Mauve stuck her brush in a tin and sat down on the concrete. She seemed exhausted.

'It's the warmest picture I've ever seen,' said Kerrie. She hadn't meant to speak her thought.

Mauve looked wary, then pleased, her expressions colliding with each other like the colours on her canvas.

'You're Kerrie,' she said.

Kerrie nodded, wondering what Sarah had told her.

'It's yours,' said Mauve. 'If you want it. I'm fed up with it.'

'The painting?' asked Kerrie, stunned.

'Put it in your new home,' said Mauve. 'Wherever it is. I'll finish those last bits later.' She wiped her brush and turned her back on everyone.

Shell grinned at Kerrie. She never could resist the glamour of adventure.

Janis looked uneasy though. She would have some doubts about all this, Kerrie knew. Janis liked to lay out every detail of an escapade in her head first. She liked to be able to see everything set out clearly and ordered in the same way that she would organize her pens, rubbers, mascots and jotters on her desks at school. It was a painstaking ritual that infuriated teachers.

But this wasn't an adventure or an escapade like any other. This was Kerrie's life they were messing around with. As the weight of this fact struck, Kerrie had a sudden sensation that she was paper thin. The slightest wind or spot of rain and she would blow away, dissolve. Kerrie made herself listen to Janis, who was asking

Mauve how anybody could actually manage to live up on a rooftop.

Mauve didn't answer at first. She just looked Janis over as if she was a bit of painting that hadn't turned out too well. Janis carried on asking a string of questions. Mauve put her chin in her hand, staring at the ground. Then she stretched slowly like a cat.

'Are you lot messing about or is there a real problem here?' Mauve stared at Sarah. 'I'm not a novelty act, see.'

Sarah looked distraught, an odd expression for Sarah. Now everyone was staring at Kerrie. She opened her mouth.

'My gran died.'

Nothing else came out.

'Right,' said Mauve.

Kerrie could feel Mauve studying her face and felt her mood change like the wash of a warm wind. Mauve began to talk in a rush.

'OK, I'll tell you how it is. I don't live up here, though it sometimes feels that way 'cause I'm here all the time. When the weather's fine I even bring up a sleeping bag so's I can catch the light at dawn. I stay with my pal, Ruth, and her baby on the top floor. I'm on the couch but it's a sight better than a hostel or bed-and-breakfast land. I've got a whole roof.'

'But there's a boy lives up here,' said Shell.

'Oh, sure,' said Mauve. 'Skip's got himself organized. Totally.'

'See, we need to get Kerrie organized,' Shell

continued. She would sleep easier tonight if she knew that Kerrie's immediate future was settled.

Mauve had taken up her brush again and made a broad slash of emerald across the heart of the sunset. She's ruined it, thought Kerrie, what did she do that for? But as she stared, something seemed to shift in her vision and Kerrie saw that it wasn't ruined at all.

Mauve held her brush steady in the air and nodded, still intent on her canvas. In the deepening dark, the green slash held in the torch beam seemed to intensify second by second.

'Well, I can tell you how Skip survives and you see how it grabs you. It's hard but Skip wouldny live anywhere else now. No' that he's got much choice.' The girl's matter-of-fact tone was at odds with her trance-like preoccupation with the painting. Then she shrugged and looked at Kerrie. 'But maybe you don't either.'

Mauve seemed to exist on waves, one minute thrown up on the breakers of colour she had created on canvas, the next sucked back on an undertow into the real world. She seemed at ease with this ebb and flow but Kerrie found it disconcerting. Just when she seemed once again to have forgotten their presence, Mauve turned with a grin that took away her fierce look and made her look like a pixie or an elf, tiny as she was with her mantle of jewellery.

'It's no' that bad. There's a lot worse nightmares in the world.'

'Tell me how Skip lives,' said Kerrie, trying to hold

Mauve's gaze. 'I . . . I'm just not sure. I canny imagine it.'

Mauve put down her paintbrush and stepped outside the torch-beam, resigned to spending some time exclusively in the real world.

'Practical survival. Well, he cooks from tins on a wee gas stove or he goes to the soup kitchen in the church hall for a hot meal. Though that'd be out, if they're looking for you. Anyway, you could survive with a stove, tins of things. Then, Skip collects rainwater in there.'

She pointed to a large, rusted oil-drum.

'There's never any shortage of that. And the sheds are solid, no windows so they've no draughts, though they're dripping with damp. But so are the flats so you'll be used to that.'

'What about baths?' asked Janis grimly. 'And toilets.'

'She could have a bath in that,' suggested Shell, meaning the oil-drum.

'You find ways,' said Mauve. 'Every now and then Skip sneaks down to my pal's for a bath when she's away out.'

'But I'd need money and food and . . . lots of things. What am I supposed to do all day?' argued Kerrie.

'You'd find something – or go daft.' Again Mauve broke into her pixie grin, the light from the city on her face.

'Me and Skip, for instance, we've got our business. I call it Sound and Vision. He busks and I sell my

30

paintings. Well, try to. But some days we make a bundle of money.'

'Kerrie plays guitar!'

'She's brill,' said Shell. 'She's in our band, the Restless Souls.'

Kerrie flushed, glad of the dark. 'I'm OK,' she muttered.

Her guitar-playing was the one thing, other than Gran, that Kerrie had always felt sure about, not considering herself clever like Janis or wild like Shell with her crazy ideas. Nor did she have Sarah's hard sense of her own self. Just carrying her guitar gave Kerrie confidence, an identity. Playing it made her feel more like herself than anything else in the world. The others were always teasing her about the way she would wrap the guitar in an old piece of red velvet curtain before she tucked it into its black leather bag. 'Just like it was a wee baby princess,' Shell said.

But Gran understood right away.

'Your grandpa felt just the same about playing in his folk band,' she'd say.

And she'd sit and nod encouragingly as Kerrie struggled through new chords and scraps of songs even though she couldn't have liked the offbeat music of the Restless Souls. Kerrie always felt soothed by Gran's quiet approval as she pretended to read her library book. Kerrie guessed she was really dreaming about Grandpa and the old days.

Everyone was waiting now for Kerrie to decide about the roof. Yet there was still something she had to know.

'Won't he – Skip – mind me, um, muscling in like this? On his territory?' she said at last.

'Oh, I wouldn't bother about him. It's no' his roof,' said Mauve. Then she whispered, 'He's dead shy, that's all.'

So Mauve knew he was there.

'Anyway,' said Janis, who had by now decided to back the plan, 'we'll all be looking after you, bringing you up food and stuff.'

'Course,' said Shell. 'You'll be our official charity. We'll have a fund every week and buy your shopping.'

It seemed that everybody else had made up their minds. Kerrie wished things weren't developing so fast; she couldn't think. She put her last obstacle before them. 'They'd look for me up here. Right away.'

'No' if we tell them you've run away off to London,' said Shell. 'To live in cardboard city and beg at the Houses of Parliament and drift into a life of crime and drugs and disease.'

The others looked at her askance.

'I saw it all on a TV programme,' she assured them. 'Terrible.' She touched Kerrie's arm. 'Aw, Kerrie, this'd be all right, not some grotty nightmare like that. And you'd still be near us. I don't know what else we can do,' she ended quietly.

Kerrie looked up at the crowded sky. Just above the rooftop fence a star pulsed red. Everyone was waiting for her to speak but she could only watch the star, her mind a blank as to what she should do.

Kerrie gripped the rooftop fence. The tower block,

stuck fast to the earth, was her only anchor. The red star-pulse seemed to pull her, warm yet threatening; if she loosened her grip for an instant Kerrie knew she would free-fall from the earth into that endless ocean of sky.

Something grabbed her and tried to shake her free of the fence.

'Kerrie!' Shell's voice was sharp. She looked frightened. 'Don't get weird,' she snapped. Shell always got snappy when she was scared.

'I'm just thinking,' Kerrie muttered, as the world resettled itself. She stole a glance up at the sky but a large cloud had sailed over the red star. She unlocked her fingers from the fence and tried a step or two. The earth felt sure and steady once more.

But what was she to do? Say no, she couldn't stay on a rooftop. Then what? Back to Mum? Foster parents or a children's home if she kicked up a real fuss? London, running away, was just a joke. Whatever her choice, she'd be far away from Shell and the others which would be unbearable. And too far away from Gran somehow.

'Well, I'll try it. I'll give it a shot. I just don't fancy being trapped up here till I'm sixteen.' Kerrie screwed up her face. 'Bored out my tiny mind. I'll get recognized if I go down to the ground.'

'Disguise yourself,' said Shell. 'We'll buy you a false beard.'

'Aye, you could,' said Janis. 'No' a beard, you

dumpling. But you could cut your hair and change your style.'

She looked at Mauve's armour of brooches and caught sight of the time on the large watch-face that Mauve wore pinned to her waistcoat.

'Yoiks, ten o'clock, I've had it. I was warned.'

Kerrie's eyes were sore with exhaustion, her head felt too heavy for her neck to support for very much longer.

'I don't want to go back there,' she said.

The house would be full of people by now. Like Phil, Mum's latest.

'Stay at mine. I'll get Mum to phone and tell them,' said Shell.

'Mauve, can we meet you up here in the morning?' asked Sarah who, as usual, had been observing events in silence.

'Sure,' said Mauve.

Kerrie hung back as the others left, their footsteps echoing as they ran along the corridor to the lifts. The rooftop was black and silent, apart from the hard circle of light made by Mauve's torch. Like a radio left humming in the corner of a room, the city was only a vague background noise.

Kerrie peered at the strange shapes and shadows of the rooftop litter. A breath stuck in her throat as a pile of tarpaulin came to life and shifted its position. The tarpaulin coughed and Kerrie saw it was the boy, hunched up on the ground, huddled into his huge coat. He was staring at her through a mess of dark hair that fell over his eyes. Kerrie hesitated for a moment. Then as the boy continued with his silent stare she lost her nerve and opened the door behind her, escaping into the yellow light of the lift corridor.

Which way?

'Any hair mousse, Kerrie-cookie? I'm a flop without it,' Mum called from the other side of the bedroom door.

Kerrie was pretending not to have heard but Mum came in all the same. She sat down on the edge of the bed and made a face at her reflection in the dressing-table mirror as she fingered the heavy fringe she was forever trying to plump up with mousses, gels and backcombing.

It took up huge chunks of Mum's life, that fringe. Kerrie thought she looked younger, plain in a boyish kind of way, with her face clean of make-up and her fringe all straight and lank over one eye, the sides and back cropped short and sleek. This month Mum's hair was mahogany red which gave her head a strange pink aura in daylight.

Kerrie-cookie. Mum hadn't called her that stupid name in years. Kerrie looked up from the rigorous guitar polishing she had begun in an attempt to take her mind off the funeral tomorrow morning. Mum was watching her closely. She looked tense, all tight round her mouth and eyes.

'What do you want?' Kerrie sighed.

Mum's face flickered. 'Just some mousse – oh, Kerrie.'

Mum put her face in her hands and rubbed her eyebrows with the tips of her fingers. Here we go, Kerrie told herself, and waited. But Mum just sniffled a bit, then straightened up and looked at Kerrie with rubbed, raw-looking eyes.

'I've been a rotten mum, eh?'

Kerrie decided she wasn't playing, whatever the game was. With a nail, she began to pick out the tune of 'Incey Wincey Spider' on the guitar.

'I'm not expecting you to understand, Kerrie. You got stuck in the middle of it all. You were just a kiddy.'

This was new. What was she up to? Kerrie wondered.

'It's taken the feet from me, your gran dying like that. I always thought she'd be there, strong as a rock, picking up the pieces after me and my messes.'

'Like me, you mean. I was one of your messes.' Kerrie made the words clear and sharp.

'You? Oh.' Mum was flummoxed by that. She got up and found a jar of blue hair gel in amongst the clutter on Kerrie's dressing table and massaged in a great dollop.

That would have lasted me a week, thought Kerrie.

'I'm just thirty-six, Kerrie, and everything I've done I've mucked up,' Mum was saying. 'I've stayed away so

I wouldn't muck you up any more. Mum wouldn't let me do that. She loved you too much.'

Kerrie jumbled up a run of notes in 'Pop Goes the Weasel', her eyes blurring over, her throat tightening. She curled her toes and her tongue.

Leave me alone, alone.

Alone.

Kerrie sounded the word in her head. She saw the roof, bleak and brilliant with Mauve's chalk designs. And far beyond, cluttered with stumps of tower blocks, with spires and tenement roofs, she saw the city horizon spelling out the word ALONE in still, grey lettering.

'Kerrie, I want to make things right for us,' said Mum. 'Your gran would want that. I sat up all night thinking, one day I'll die too and what a mess I've made. I'm still young. Well,' Mum shrugged and smiled, 'not totally over the hill. But there's just the two of us now. I'll sort myself out and we'll make it work, eh, Kerrie?'

Kerrie wriggled her fingers in the soft, green pile of the bedroom carpet. Her head felt light and clear, she was all a-tingle as if she'd just plugged herself into an electric socket. Her vision was so sharp she could see the individual shiny strands of fibre that wound together to make up each tuft of carpet. There was a winding leaf pattern that ran in a darker shade through the pale green. Kerrie followed a trail in the pattern with her finger until the pattern split into fronds, each of which split into further and further fronds. Her finger dithered at the split in the pattern. Which way, which way?

'It'll be different this time, Kerrie,' said Mum. 'Promise.'

Kerrie studied Mum's face, the green eyes and the features that so unnervingly reflected her own, and Gran's. There were photos of the three of them as young girls set alongside each other in Gran's photograph album and it was as if the same light-eyed, dark-haired girl had time-travelled through the generations.

But when Kerrie smiled it was Dad's wide, steady smile, the one that she saw in occasional, flashing dreams of him.

Strangely, Kerrie's memories of Dad seemed to have disappeared even though she had been nine, old enough to remember, when he left. It was as if he'd packed them up and taken them away with him. But Kerrie could see the horrible times after he left until Gran rescued her as if through a pane of glass.

Times when Mum's crying would waken her in the night. In the morning Mum would still be dead to the world on the living-room couch with the debris of a whisky binge all around. Kerrie would leave for school after a breakfast of dry cornflakes because there was no milk, no tea, no bread, nothing else she could find to eat.

There were times when Mum seemed to hate Kerrie as a reminder of Dad. Afterwards, she'd try to make up. She'd come in with half a sweet shop rustling in her bag and seemed to think Kerrie would forget all the nastiness after a dose of chocolate and cola, a new release from the video shop and a couple of arm-numbing hugs.

Then came the nights that Kerrie woke to raised voices. Mum and the man's – the man who was sometimes sprawled on the couch watching TV when she got home from school; the man who pretended Kerrie wasn't there.

Then one morning Mum was gone.

Kerrie had sat down among a litter of bottles and cans on the living-room floor, numb and blank. After a while she phoned Gran and told her everything. Everything that she and Mum, like a couple of guilty criminals, had been hiding all these months. And Gran, furious and upset, had come at once and rescued her.

'Don't look at me so fierce,' said Mum, interrupting Kerrie's thoughts. She gave a hard little laugh. 'You're just like him when you look at me angry like that.'

'Will he ever come back?' The words were out of Kerrie's mouth before she could stop them. Mum stared at her.

A loud rap sounded and they both jumped. The bedroom door swung open and Phil, Mum's new boyfriend, stood there. Gran's purse was in his hand.

'I'm just away down to the off-sales. We're running short on supplies. Whisky for you, Lynne, and vodka, gin, and a ton of beer for me, ha, ha. Should do it, eh? Oh, and Coke and crisps for this one.' Phil winked at Kerrie. 'We'll look after you, pal, don't you worry. Aye, and we'll give the old lady a good send off.'

Phil's shoes crushed a frond of the green carpet pattern as he stood grinning sloppily at Mum, shifting from one foot to the other.

Kerrie stood up, cold with anger.

'That's my gran's purse,' she shouted at Mum. 'He's rifled Gran's purse for money so the two of you can get blootered.'

Phil disappeared. Mum turned to the dressing-table mirror and began frantically backcombing her fringe. She had put too much gel on, it looked like a bird's-nest.

'Nothing's different,' said Kerrie. 'You're all talk. And if you'd been around more you might've noticed Gran wasny strong. You might've seen she was ill and done something.'

As she, Kerrie, should have.

Kerrie took the lidless pot of hair gel and threw it against a wall. Sticky blue dollops spattered the bedspread, the guitar and the carpet. Mum turned round with her wide-eyed, childlike look. She rubbed at some blue gel that had landed on the leg of her jeans. She looked miserable, avoiding Kerrie's eyes.

'I'll sort things after the funeral,' she said.

'Sort him then. Get rid of him,' Kerrie demanded.

Mum said nothing, just stood there.

'Well, I would,' she said at last. 'If that's what it takes.'

'Sure you would,' muttered Kerrie. She turned her back on Mum and, leaning on the window sill, stared out at clouds and the windows of neighbouring tower blocks until she heard Mum sigh, defeated. The bedroom door shut softly and Kerrie was alone.

It was a clear blue day and Kerrie could see right across to the still, crooked fingers of the dockyard cranes by the river and the tower blocks that ringed the city in clusters like an enclosure of modern-day monoliths.

Mauve was finishing off the painting she'd promised Kerrie. On the rooftop behind them there was a bustle of activity around one of the sheds.

'Y'know, I hardly ever noticed the view from our flat. The windies are too high up and anyway you look straight into other people's flats,' said Kerrie.

In a way, it could be a brilliant place to live. On days like this or on wide sparkly nights you'd feel like you were a part of the whole world.

'They reckon it stops us all jumping out,' said Sarah, who had flopped down beside them on the ground. Sweat shone on her face. 'High windies, y'know.'

Kerrie laughed and Sarah looked pleased with herself. They had all been uncomfortable with the stiff, dazed expression on Kerrie's face these last few days.

A plane flew deafeningly low to one side of them. Its shuddering roar became high-pitched screaming as the engines reversed to brake. The plane landed just out of sight beyond the ring of tower blocks, a great rumble indicating its touchdown.

Mauve made a face at the noise. 'Progress,' she said. 'All those brilliant old buildings, the domes and church spires. And all these big ugly lumps of cement. There's a way round them in paintings. Like if you use the sun on all that glass, a blazing wall of fire. But there's never a way round them in real life.'

'Do you ever paint the mountains?' asked Kerrie. She'd first noticed these this morning from the opposite side of the roof. 'I never knew there were mountains as close. We faced the other way.'

'They're just hills,' said Mauve. 'Real mountains are much further up. I'd like to check out that kind of scenery some day, get out the city and away into the wilds. I think I could do something different with all that.'

'We're about ready,' Shell called from the other side of the roof. She ran over, red with excitement, and yanked Kerrie out of her daydreams about the wild places she had never seen that lay far beyond the city.

Kerrie tested her new bed. It was made from layer upon layer of newspaper, covered by further layers of blankets. Over this was a sleeping bag, then more blankets and quilts.

'It *should* be warm enough,' said Janis.

'She'll probably die under the weight of it,' grinned Shell, her expression withering as she remembered Kerrie's gran.

'Think I'm having a heart attack,' wheezed Sarah as she crashed in the door, her arms straining with boxes. Shell winced.

'That's us then. Finito,' said Janis, and they all crammed into the small room to have a look.

43

In two corners thick candles burned, wavering a warm light up the crumbling plaster. Posters covered the worst patches of the walls. Beside the bed there was a radio-cassette, tapes, magazines and books. Kerrie's guitar was propped on the wall next to these. In the opposite corner from the bed was a tiny kitchen area. Shell had knocked up a set of shelves made out of crates that lay around the rooftop, and stacked on these were tins and jars and plates. Next to this was an old plastic baby bath and a gas-burner which Sarah mysteriously had turned up with.

'It's amazing,' said Kerrie. 'Ta, you lot.'

'You're not just being polite now are you, Kerrie?' said Shell, puffing out her cheeks and blinking in her cruel imitation of Margaret. 'Oh, where's the surprise?'

Sarah lifted something out of one of the boxes she had brought up and Kerrie gasped as something warm and furry landed on her jumper. A black kitten lunged at her chin.

'*And* new guitar strings,' said Shell, chucking them on the bed. 'My brother's always losing them.'

Kerrie grinned at her, struggling to keep hold of the kitten.

'Well then,' said Shell.

Kerrie knew Shell was trying to avoid mentioning the funeral. She tried to sound composed, as if she knew what was happening. 'I'll leave my note and slip up here when they're all back at Gran's. After the funeral.'

'While they're having a booze-up.' Shell shook her

head. 'I've never understood that bit. Callous. If I die, I want you all greeting your eyes out. No partying.'

'They'll probably no' even notice you're missing till the morning,' said Sarah.

'And by then you'd be well on your way to London,' grinned Shell. 'They'll never even glance up here.'

'Good stuff,' said Janis, 'but we'd better stay clear of this place for a while, just in case.'

Shell considered. 'This is Tuesday. I'll see you tomorrow, Kerrie, at – at the church. Then I'd better leave it till the weekend. You'll be all right by yourself?' She fidgeted a drumbeat with the kitten's tail.

Kerrie nodded, wondering whether she would.

'She's no' by herself. Mauve's here,' reminded Sarah. 'And Skip.'

Kerrie thought uneasily about the boy. He hadn't come near her yet.

'At least there's enough food,' said Janis. 'Even for Kerrie.'

It was clear they were all feeling uncomfortable now that they faced the reality of leaving Kerrie alone on the roof. Until now none of it had seemed very real, as if they had been playing at dens like they did just a couple of years ago.

'Get practising,' said Shell, handing Kerrie her guitar. 'You were way out of tune on Saturday.'

'Me?' Kerrie began, then realized Shell was winding her up, as usual. She laughed to herself. As usual. Nothing would ever be as usual again.

'I think I'll stick up here on my own for a while,' said

Kerrie. She needed some time alone to become familiar with her new home. One day at a time, she told herself, that's all I'll think about.

It was the only funeral Kerrie had ever attended and she had come to it blankly, refusing to imagine what it might be like.

'It was beautiful,' Margaret whispered to one person after another, as the crowd left the graveside.

Kerrie had a salty taste like blood in the back of her mouth from the heartbeat in her throat. She had stood alone, ignoring the commotion around the coffin at the graveside, intent on folding a shiny, emerald-green sweet paper that she'd found in one of Gran's pockets into the tiniest of parcels. Almost the worst part of the last few days had been helping Margaret to sort out Gran's clothes to make up into parcels for Oxfam and Help the Aged. Kerrie had found sweet papers stuffed away in the pockets of coats and cardigans, hordes of crinkly paper jewels, still smelling of toffee or mint or fudge.

And then, in the jewellery box that sat on Gran's dressing-table, Margaret had found the letter. *To Kerrie*, it said on the envelope in Gran's old-fashioned, looping script. Kerrie had taken it to her room to read, but after a few lines she shoved the letter back in its envelope. She was choked with angry tears. Gran's letter was all about Mum.

Kerrie could have torn it in pieces. Gran had left her

nothing, nothing that was any use, just a letter full of Mum.

Mum had separated herself from the thinning line of black coats at the graveside. She came over, took one of Kerrie's cold hands and rubbed it warm between her gloved ones. Kerrie saw it was the tiger-pattern gloves. She used to think they were real tiger paws when she was small, and would pin them down under mattresses and table legs so that they wouldn't come chasing after her when she wasn't looking. She chewed her lip and looked at Mum.

'We could be a wee family. The three of us,' whispered Mum.

Phil appeared at Mum's other side. He took one of her tiger paws in his hand. He had worn a pink carnation and a pink tie to go with it. Pink socks too, Kerrie noted, as if he was at a wedding.

'What a great old lady.' Phil shook his head.

Kerrie put her head down and walked off. He'd never met her.

'She blew it, Gran,' Kerrie whispered, the wind whipping the words away. 'She might have left that creep out of it.'

And then, from nowhere, the memory had come. She was on the waterfront with Dad. The dockyard and the cranes were across the river. He was talking about the great ships once built here that crossed the oceans to faraway countries. His face was sparkling with the thought of it but all Kerrie could see was the ships being sucked downriver like great floundering whales into the endlessness of the oceans. She had wanted to hide her face in Dad's scratchy jacket, at the idea that there was anything so huge and empty in the world as an ocean. And to be set loose on it, with no anchor to anything that was fixed, must be the worst thing in the world.

Kerrie had begun to cry and Dad was angry, saying she was just like her mother. He seemed to stay angry after that, his face dulled by it, until one day he disappeared into the great emptiness as she guessed he would, and she knew that his face would be sparkling again with the reflection of the sun on the water.

Kerrie had never let herself think of him adrift like a speck of dust in the universe. Not till now, standing in a cemetery with familiar faces drifting by that did not look at her.

Maybe, Kerrie suddenly thought, maybe on a clear day the view from the rooftop would stretch as far as the sea.

Part two
The roof

Skip and the sparkly

Kerrie had heaved and rolled and shoved a large oil-drum full of rainwater until it sat against the wall of her shed. That was better, she nodded, straightening her aching back. Now she had a handy source of water. If she mostly ate fruit or things out of tins and packets she could save messing up so much crockery and cutlery. And it was easier just to wear the same dirty jeans each day, changing about layers of T-shirts and jumpers. That only left underwear to wash out. Her long hair was a problem but this morning she had braided it tight into her head so that she could forget about it for a while.

'You should've waited and I'd've given you a hand.'

Kerrie jumped at the unexpected sound of a voice. It was Mauve, up for a painting session. She came up to the roof most days but you never knew when to expect her. Mauve always brought up sandwiches and a treat of some kind – a discount bag of yesterday's scones or doughnuts from the baker's – and insisted Kerrie share them in return for several mugs of tea.

Kerrie would bring out her gas-burner and heat up a pan of rainwater while Mauve set out her little paint pots and her brushes. After they'd eaten, Kerrie would strum at a new song on her guitar or make warm, safe burrows into books while Mauve lost herself in the world she was creating on her canvas.

Mauve was odd company. She drifted in and out of conversation to the rhythm of her moods. At first Kerrie had tried to break through Mauve's trance-like spells, curious about her strange new friend. Where did Mauve live before? How had she become an artist? What about her family? Kerrie wanted to know. But it was like asking a zombie that only breathed, blinked and painted.

'Oh, I don't know,' Mauve would sigh when Kerrie's persistence eventually got to her. Or she would answer in bewildering fragments. From piecing together the fragments, Kerrie was sure that Mauve had known trouble, too. She seemed to have flitted from patch to patch all through her life with no notion of where she might land up next. Exactly why this had been, Kerrie could only guess. Painting, she saw, was Mauve's sure and steady rock. As Gran had been Kerrie's rock.

'That boy is seriously bugging me,' Kerrie burst out now, as Mauve tried out a streak of orange on her canvas. Again and again, Kerrie would look over her shoulder to find the boy watching her from his end of the roof. Yet no sooner would she catch his eye than he would shrink back into his shed like a snail into its shell.

'He'll come round in time,' was all Mauve said, splashing lumps of colour all over her canvas.

Yet for Kerrie time had become a problem, a vast open space that she struggled to map out: this lump of time to sleep in, this to make music in, this to train up Restless as the world's first kitten to perform death-defying tricks on the top of an oil-drum. Sometimes she would play circuses all night, with Restless starring in a torch beam, and Shell would arrive with supplies of food and magazines to find her fast asleep at four o'clock in the afternoon.

Already, after just a week or so, Kerrie was wondering if she could stick it out on the roof.

Last Sunday, Shell and Janis had arrived with chicken legs, roast potatoes and various other scavenged leftovers, along with the latest news of the hunt for Kerrie that had been in all the papers and on the Scottish TV news. Kerrie had been alone for most of the previous day and a sensation of separateness had descended on her, so intense she felt an invisible bubble had sliced down between her and the outside world.

Sealed inside the bubble, all Kerrie's senses had grown supercharged. The distant drum of the traffic in the streets had become a roaring in her ears, its vibrations made tremors in her bones. Kerrie felt every drop of moisture in the air gather in a damp cloud inside the bubble and lightly drench her. She started to count the church spires on the horizon that were gathering up like an army of spears.

When Shell and Janis arrived Kerrie knew she'd have

to tell them she couldn't stay on the roof any longer or she'd end up totally loopy.

'They're saying you're emotionally disturbed because of your gran and your mum's been in the *Sunday Mail* pleading with you to come home. It's real dramatic stuff. D'you hear me, Kerrie?'

Kerrie reran Shell's words in her head. Mum, playing the tragedy queen. She was good at that.

'How much did that earn her, I wonder?' Kerrie muttered.

'She was dripping with tears in the photo,' said Janis.

Kerrie felt the familiar odd mix of emotions as she pictured Mum, tears pouring down her face, surrounded by photographers. Mum in tears – that image had the power to dredge up all the bad old memories again. Life with Mum could easily be worse than this, Kerrie told herself. At least up here on the rooftop she wasn't trapped in that nerve-wracking rollercoaster life.

And there was something uncomfortably satisfying in knowing that at long last she had Mum's attention. It was punishment of a kind.

The other two were quiet as Kerrie told them that her mum was just an out-of-work actress and she, Kerrie, had no intention of playing out the happy ending that would let her pose as the doting mother all over the middle pages of the *Sunday Mail*.

Shell took a deep breath and began to backcomb Restless's fur between her fingers until he looked as if he'd had an electric shock.

'All these journalist people are getting right on my nerves,' Shell complained. 'It turns my stomach every time I see your mum in the papers and on the TV, with that Margaret and her stupid big face hanging about in the background like Mrs Glum.'

There had been police interviews for all of them, Shell went on, interrogations at school and at home, yet they still had to manage their visits to the roof and act as if they knew nothing about Kerrie's disappearance.

'Every time I'm on the phone my da's at my back,' Shell finished up. 'And I know they've been through my stuff when I'm away at school. Their eyes are hardly off me. It's the same at school with the teachers.'

Janis nodded agreement at each point in Shell's list of grievances.

'Though they'll never get you going by that photie they're using in the papers,' Shell admitted, in a fit of nervous giggles, as she studied Kerrie's face. 'It was your school one from last year when your perm went screwy and your cold sore was all over your face.'

Kerrie groaned.

'Oh, look,' Shell burst out, as she watched Kerrie chew her fingers. 'Forget what I said. If you need to stay here we'll manage, eh, Janis?'

Janis sighed. She could never muster up the effort required to block Kerrie and Shell when they were utterly set on a course of action. And she was too loyal to tell on them, Kerrie knew, even if she thought, as was clear from the look on Janis's round face, that they were completely off their heads.

'What about this boy, Skip?' asked Janis suddenly. 'Any romantic possibilities there? Is that why you're so determined to stay up here?'

Kerrie made an exaggerated yawn.

'It's no' as if he's completely ugly,' Janis continued. 'It's just that he glowers all the time.'

'He's an anti-social hermit,' said Kerrie. 'If I look at him he runs away and hides in his shed. He's a complete weirdo. Sorry, Janis.'

'Mauve says he's a poet. You wouldny expect a poet to act normal, would you?' Janis persisted.

If she was staying on the roof the problem of Skip had to be faced, Kerrie knew. Had he talked to Sarah, those few times she had visited the roof on her own before Kerrie moved up? Sarah hadn't said exactly. Maybe he hadn't talked to her either.

She would have to ask Sarah, but she hadn't been up to the roof for days. Shell said she had trouble at home but then Sarah always had trouble at home. Kerrie was sure the real problem was that Sarah couldn't handle losing the secret place she had discovered. Sarah had offered up the roof on an impulse and now it was Kerrie's. And Kerrie had Mauve as a special friend, something Sarah must have wanted, going by the awestruck manner that came over her in Mauve's presence. But whenever Sarah felt bad about something she withdrew from the world and hid in her bedroom. And Kerrie had no means of reaching her there.

So she'd have to deal with Skip on her own, Kerrie decided. His skulking presence unnerved her. Mauve insisted he had been just the same with her at first. Yet it wasn't in Kerrie's nature to be patient. Living with Gran, she had become used to getting her own way, right away too.

She wished she had gone over to him that very first night on the roof. Kerrie had closed herself up in her shed with candlelight and the soft, squirming kitten. Soon, an old-fashioned sound like wind in a chimney began and drew Restless to the door. He'd nosed at the sound and whimpered. There was something of an animal in it, like the song of whales. Kerrie blanked out the image of that lonely, lurking darkness and realized it was only the boy, Skip, playing his weird music.

Kerrie had wanted to go and sit by the boy, just to be in the presence of another human being. But she'd only opened the shed door a little to hear him better, and lay cuddling the kitten, listening to the sound of his unearthly music.

Restless snuggled up beside Kerrie at the edge of the rooftop, nibbling at the remains of her cracker and cheese spread supper. Mauve was gone and none of the gang had managed a visit today. It was unlikely anyone would come up now. Kerrie fluffed up the kitten's fur to dust off some chalk.

'You're every colour of the rainbow,' she told him. He was forever rolling about in Mauve's floor designs, lying on his back, paws waggling as if he was running through the air. Kerrie thought he was trying to catch a passing bird or a cloud.

Suddenly the boy scuffed past on the way over to his shed, not seeing Kerrie in the dusk light. He'd been down to the ground.

'Come on, Restless. Your bedtime,' Kerrie whispered.

With the kitten settled in the shed, she went over to Skip's side of the roof, her guitar under her arm. It might give them a point of contact. The boy was hunched up in his coat beside the fence, twisting an object that he held up towards the gathering lights of the city. When he heard Kerrie's footsteps he shoved the object into his pocket, turned and glared.

Kerrie had seen the object spark like glitter or fire. She was prepared for his glare, and stared him out.

Janis was right, he wasn't ugly. He had quite a delicate, stark white face. But the perpetual glare made a gash of his mouth and black pits of his eyes. He was about the same age as herself.

The boy looked away first. Kerrie began to strum her guitar, feeling increasingly foolish, until she found the chords she wanted. Then she played an impression of his music. It sounded less lonely, warmer on the guitar.

Nothing. No response at all. The boy just stared out over the city.

'So you're not gonny talk to me. Not ever.' Kerrie was glad her voice had come out strong. 'Oh well. Stick you.'

She walked back over to her own territory, casually swinging her guitar in case he was watching.

Then . . .

The mouth-organ began its solitary shiver.

Kerrie left her shed door open, snuggling Restless close inside the sleeping-bag.

It was communication, of a sort.

From then on Skip would sit watching the sky and the city all day on the far edge of the roof. He kept his distance, ignoring her, but at least he'd stopped hiding. Occasionally he would scribble things in a tatty notepad. When Mauve wasn't around he occasionally sniffed at a crisp bag he kept in one of his huge coat pockets. And always, after the glue, he spun the strange sparkly object on the ground.

Once, Mauve had caught him with the glue and dragged him by the hair into his shed. Kerrie started to curliewurlie as she heard Mauve yell and fling things. After a while she emerged to work up a storm on her canvas.

Much later, Skip surfaced. He came over and held out a paper bag. For the first time he looked straight at Kerrie without the glare. Kerrie froze, but Mauve was lost in the stabbing rhythm of her paintbrush.

Skip deposited the bag and sauntered back to his shed. Kerrie stared at it and felt sick. She picked it up and went over to her own shed. Heart hammering, she brought the bag to her face, and sniffed. The smell was sweet and golden. She must be hallucinating already. Kerrie looked inside and giggled. She'd been sniffing a bag of toffees.

*

'So what is it? That shiny toy he's always spinning?' Kerrie had asked Mauve as they gnawed their way through Skip's bag of toffee caramels.

Mauve just shrugged and said it was safer than glue.

'Why's he need a toy at his age?' Kerrie persisted.

'Same as anyone. What's a guitar or books or a kitten? They're just toys.'

'Och. But me and Restless have good fun. I canny see what the fun is in spinning a sparkly circle on the ground for hours every day. Well, can you?'

Mauve shrugged. 'He says he sees things in it. Pictures, ideas. It helps him write his poems.'

'They must be weird poems,' said Kerrie.

'What's weird? He's just lonely inside himself. Skip's had a hard time just keeping his head together. Even if he does slip up from time to time.'

Mauve sooked her paintbrush. 'I'd say we've all got a lot in common.'

'Skip. Gonny get me a newspaper?' Kerrie called as, squashed and yawning, the boy finally emerged from his shed. Kerrie had been waiting for him all morning and was beside him before he quite knew it, shoving a few coins into one of his coat pockets. 'I just want to see if I'm in it today,' she grinned.

He never looked at her, just turned and walked on. But Kerrie had seen a flicker on his face that might have been a smile.

*

In one hand he held the sparkly disc. In the other his tatty notepad. The boy stood in her doorway.

'Sorry, didn't hear you knock.' Kerrie was crisp and polite. He hadn't.

Ignores me all this time, she fumed, then comes barging in at midnight. He had some cheek.

Skip was looking at her with the same flicker in his face she'd seen this morning.

'I brought over my sparkly.'

His voice was gruff as if he didn't use it much. The sound of it seemed to startle him even more than it did her. Kerrie wondered what on earth she was supposed to say. She'd better say something quick; he looked like he could just turn and go.

'Right. Well, come in then.'

Hardly encouraging, but what did he expect when he'd taken her totally by surprise? Then, she had done the same to him, hadn't she, barging up on to his roof without warning.

Skip shuffled in and stooped down beside the bed-side candle. He placed the sparkly under its light. Then he spun it. Kerrie caught her breath as the dimness of the room scattered. Brilliant fireflies darted from the sparkly, stars exploded, rainbow lightning forked and spiked. Restless tried to pounce on the coloured lights and Kerrie held him back.

'It's – it's utterly crazy. You could watch it for hours.'

'I do,' said Skip.

'So you do.'

Kerrie picked up the disc when it was finally still. It

was slightly larger than her hand and felt metallic. Underneath, she felt the tiny point in its centre that the sparkly spun on. Every fraction that she tilted it, the candlelight changed its colours and patterns. Blazing red and gold crashed greens and blues, then tinted to icy shades of purple and silver. She handed it back at last to save it from Restless.

'And I brought a poem,' said Skip.

'Oh. Ta.'

Once again, Kerrie was at a loss. She took the tatty notepad that he held out to her and saw an explosion of words scattered all over the page. Then she saw that there was a kind of a pattern to the scatter. It reminded her of something. Skip was looking at her edgily. She floundered for a response. It was unlike any poem she'd ever seen.

'What's it about?' she asked.

'I kinda collect thoughts in my head and then I write them down the way they burst in. You think it's daft then?'

The scowl was back on his face again.

'Nah, I like it,' said Kerrie. 'It's weird. It's like looking at the sparkly.' She said this hastily, in desperation that he might switch off from her again but Skip's face had creased into a soft, delighted grin.

'D'you really think so? That's just what I think. It's when I look in my sparkly that I find a poem.' He shook his head, nonplussed. 'Imagine you seeing that.'

Kerrie was just as delighted that her flash of inspiration was so well-received. She stared at this new, smiling Skip. He seemed a world away from the boy on the roof this morning. For the first time she could see his eyes clearly and was surprised that they were a soft mud-brown, not black.

'You know, you're like Sarah right enough. Her face cracks like that when she smiles 'cause she hardly ever does, too.'

Skip rubbed his head with his hand, shy once more.

'Where'd you get your sparkly then?' Kerrie was determined that the conversation would not dry up.

'Well . . .' He looked at her warily. 'I suppose I stole it. But I'm no' a thief,' he added quickly. 'No' a real one. I only steal if I really need something, like if I'm hungry.'

Kerrie said nothing. She didn't want to point out that you couldn't eat a sparkly.

'But this was different, see,' he argued with her silence. 'I was in this shop doorway one day, it was pouring with rain and I just saw them all sitting in the windie. I was looking at them for ages and ages. "Explore the infinite mesmeric pattern of light in the spinning laser disc," it said on the packet. "The powerful radiance of the disc will enhance your own protective aura."'

Skip recited this slowly, in a sinister accent. Kerrie forced herself not to giggle.

'I thought they were like bits of magic, like they'd fallen off a rainbow or something. I thought, if I had one of them I'd be all right, it'd keep the bad times from me. I wanted one that much it was like I needed it, like I feel when . . .' He trailed off here and glared at the kitten.

He switched mood again and was suddenly matter-of-fact. 'And it's helping me come off that as well. I look at my sparkly and it makes me feel good. D'you like Mauve?' he asked, looking with approval at the sunset picture hung low on the wall beside the bed.

'Course.' Kerrie was dizzied by his switch-change moods. 'I thought that's what made you no' talk to me.'

'Nah.'

'What then?' she asked.

'Nothing.' Skip sniffed and pocketed his poem. He looked at the sparkly on the floor.

'Come on, tell me why,' she persisted.

He looked at the sparkly in concentration.

'Maybe I've been there,' he said at last. 'Maybe I didny fancy seeing somebody else there.' He stood up. 'You can keep it the night.'

All of a sudden there was a draught of wind and the strange boy was gone. Kerrie was left staring at the sparkly, feeling she had been paid a great honour, entrusted as she was with this most treasured possession. Tucking Restless securely in between herself and the wall, she stared into the quiet colours of the sparkly and gently spun it to life.

Down to the ground

Mauve was painting Skip's face on to the foreground of one of her cityscapes. He sat with the rooftop fence behind him, as Mauve transformed the fence into barbed wire in her painting. The city looked trapped behind a vicious, bristling net. Skip looked bored.

'It's an awful funny name – Skip,' Kerrie said, balancing a plate of rolls on her knees while she peeled a banana. Mauve had brought the rolls up fresh from the baker's at the foot of the hill and the smell of them had started Kerrie's stomach gurgling and groaning. She had two bananas left from a bunch Shell had brought up the other day, and Skip had donated a can of Coke. They would have quite a nice lunch, Kerrie thought happily.

Skip seemed to be ignoring her comment about his name. He was infuriatingly easy to offend.

'Unusual, I mean. Different,' Kerrie tried.

Skip spoke after a lengthy pause. 'I used to live on a building site,' he said.

'Stop fidgeting,' said Mauve.

'I have to breathe,' he protested. Skip slid his eyes to Kerrie, keeping his head perfectly still. 'That was the first place I ever ran away to. I made a shelter out of big polythene sheets that covered the piles of bricks they were building with, and I stayed there for weeks till the foreman chucked me out. But the workies were good to me. They'd let me in at their stove and give me soup and rolls 'cause I did wee odd jobs for them. They called me the Skipper Kid. Kinda like the Sundance Kid in that film. Anyway, I liked it so I kept it for my name.'

It was the first time Skip had talked to Kerrie about himself, in fact about anything at all, at such length. But, since the other night when he'd come to her shed with the sparkly, he seemed to have decided they were firm friends. He'd even told Mauve that he thought Kerrie might make a good busker.

'I'm getting sore, Mauve,' he complained now, wriggling. 'I used to pretend I was living in a wee space capsule,' he added to Kerrie.

Kerrie shuddered.

'Well, beggars like us canny be choosers about where to live. It was all right,' he added. 'Don't know how she's so fussy,' he said to Mauve. 'A kid that lives on a roof.'

'The roof kids,' said Kerrie. 'Good name for a band, that.'

Skip winked at Mauve.

'You fancy the busking then?' he asked.

'I'll see.' Kerrie was casual. 'I'll maybe come and watch.'

'Well, we were thinking about going into the town tomorrow. She could come then, eh, Mauve?'

'We were?' Mauve looked bewildered.

Kerrie realized what was happening. 'I've not said I'll do it. I'm just coming along. To see.'

'Och.'

Skip brushed away her reluctance with his hand.

'Skip!'

He sighed wearily at Mauve. 'You no' about finished yet? I'm fed up. Anyway,' he turned back to Kerrie, 'you look totally different now. Nobody'd know you.'

His switch-change thoughts were as hard to follow as his moods, thought Kerrie, fingering her new haircut, still unused to it – the feel of it anyhow as she couldn't see much of it in her hand mirror.

A few nights back Mauve's friend Ruth had gone out and her flat had been taken over for Kerrie's transformation. First Mauve, with constant interference from Shell, had cut Kerrie's long, wavy hair – rather, had shorn it till it fell in uneven wisps around Kerrie's face in a style similar to Mauve's. Kerrie had squirmed as she watched great, dark strands pile up on the floor.

'It's the only cut I know,' said Mauve, as she caught sight of Kerrie's expression. 'Looks good on you. Honest.'

Shell wanted to make Kerrie up like a white-faced Pierrot clown. There was a girl in the flats who painted herself in this fashion.

'She looks awesome,' said Shell. 'One wee purple tear on her cheek.'

67

But Kerrie liked the burnish on her skin that had come from her new outdoor life.

'I hate all that gunge. Look at the state of your Sharon,' she added.

'Oh her,' huffed Shell. 'Aye, but she's pot ugly.'

The next step had been to redesign Kerrie's clothes. Janis and Sarah had fastened items from a shoebox, in which Mauve kept her vast jewellery collection, to Kerrie's jeans and jacket. Shell, determined for some theatrical effect, had brought along a floppy crushed-velvet hat she'd picked up cheap in a charity shop. And Mauve had found a pair of earrings, set with dull green stones that were almost the colour of Kerrie's eyes.

In the full-length mirror on the wardrobe door, Kerrie had gazed at her strange new appearance and wondered what Gran would have made of it.

'Amazing,' was Shell's verdict. 'Truly amazing.'

'You gonny have a new name?' Mauve asked, as she added a silvery seahorse brooch to Kerrie's hat.

Kerrie shook her head. 'Like . . . what?'

'Pick a colour, a zodiac sign, a country you fancy,' Mauve suggested. 'Anything in the wide old universe.' She thought for a minute, appraising Kerrie with the dreamy, unblinking gaze she gave to a blank sheet of paper or canvas.

'Emerald,' she said at last. 'That's what I'd call myself if I'd eyes like yours.'

Kerrie blushed as everyone stopped their tidying away of the make-up, jewellery and hair that was scattered all over Ruth's bedroom floor to stare at her eyes. Mauve had renamed herself one day by picking a colour from one of her little pots of paint.

'I could've been Indigo or Russet,' she'd told Kerrie, after an afternoon of being pestered by questions. 'But I knew I was Mauve as soon as I tried it out.'

Mauve's old name had been a nothing name, a name for nobodies, a name you'd just throw at a baby if you couldn't be bothered, she'd said. It was only a label till she found her real name.

And that was all she would tell, until one evening when a sudden pelt of rain made Mauve abandon her canvas and run for cover into Kerrie's shed. Kerrie realized she had Mauve cornered and she'd managed at last to prise something of her past from her.

There had been foster homes, a children's home and an aunt somewhere who'd sent Mauve the odd Christmas present. The Christmas she was ten, the aunt had sent a palette of paints and Mauve had found her escape, painting herself out of the grey concrete she looked out on from the window of her dormitory in the children's home.

'You never want to go into one of those places,' she said. 'I told Skip I'd help keep him out of one if I could, and same for you.'

When, at fifteen, Mauve had finally run away from the home, she'd imagined up a new appearance for herself, a new name and a life as different as she could from the grey, regulated one at the home.

But it was different for Kerrie. All the changes of the last few weeks had been forced on her; she had been slammed out of her happy old life. A new name, on top of everything else, would be just too much.

'I'd never get used to it,' she said.

'Aw, Kerrie,' moaned Shell. 'Emerald, I mean.'

'And neither would you.' Kerrie caught her own eyes in the mirror. 'Witchy eyes,' Grandpa used to joke, when she was a little girl. 'You three must have been witches in past lives,' he'd wink, and Gran would tut, with a smile in her own green eyes.

Mauve's painting of Skip was just about done now. Kerrie sat on the roof floor, cupped her face in her hands and examined it. In the foreground Skip stood looking at the sparkly he held in his hand. Its colours glinted outwards, seeming to escape the boundaries of the painting. Mauve had captured Skip's scared-angry expression. His black hair was ruffled by a wind and just above his head an empty crisp packet blew past.

Only the eyes remained blank. Kerrie wondered if Mauve could get them right. They would change from soft brown to sunken pits of black in less than a blink.

But Mauve did something utterly unpredictable. She painted in Skip's eyes like the wild exploding stars of the sparkly.

'Aw, mental!' whooped Kerrie.

Skip loved it.

'I look like an alien,' he said contentedly. 'Don't I?'

And he sat staring at himself in the painting until it got too dark to see.

Kerrie was concentrating on holding her pose. It was

her turn to be painted and she was starting to ache with the effort of keeping still when she noticed Skip's face crumple into a delighted grin as a flutter of feathers descended on to the rooftop beside them.

'My wee pal,' said Skip. 'I've no' seen you for ages.'

He crouched and laid his arm on the ground beside the pigeon. It sauntered over to him with a drunken gait and clambered up on to his sleeve.

Skip began speaking gibberish to the pigeon who fixed an orange eye on the middle distance. Kerrie spluttered and Mauve laughed soundlessly at her painting.

'What have you brought me the day then, my wee pet?' Skip asked the pigeon.

The bird ruffled out its feathers and flexed a foot. Carefully, Skip lifted a wing and felt around its legs. He fiddled for a moment while the pigeon gazed without interest around the rooftop. Then Skip lowered his arm to the ground and the pigeon set off on an unsteady ramble around the shed.

Skip unravelled a long, thin strip of paper.

'What is it?' Kerrie asked, forgetting to pose. She knew it was news of some kind from Doo, the old man who lived with his pigeons on the next roof. Kerrie had heard Mauve and Skip talk about him, had seen the clouds of pigeons on the other roof and the man's little red hat bobbing among them. But it was only when she found Skip untying a tiny note from the leg of a pigeon one day that she discovered Doo sent over regular bulletins by pigeon post: odd bits of poems for Skip, weather reports for Mauve's painting, gossip about the pigeons or just his thoughts. Kerrie had asked Skip to say hello from her via a pigeon and in return Doo had sent her a poem:

> *On The Roof*
> *Wonder*
> *Evolves*
> *Life*
> *Connects*
> *Only*
> *Misery*
> *Ends*

'But when?' Kerrie had written back.

'In the end,' was Doo's response.

'I asked him for a weather report for our busking,' Skip was saying now, reading Doo's tiny writing. 'He's got three new arrivals and Scooby's had a wee wing problem, he says. That right, Scooby?'

The pigeon ignored him and pecked around Mauve's paintbrushes.

'He's been getting hassle.'

Skip's tone had changed.

'From the polis?' asked Mauve. 'Have they no' got more important things to do, like catch criminals?'

Skip was silent, studying the long strip of paper.

'Naw, it's worse. Headbangers breaking on to his roof and having crazy parties. Ah, I don't believe it.'

Skip's eyes deepened to black. He read some more

and then turned and punched the mesh fence, directing an outburst of foul language towards the ground.

'People,' he finished, shaking his head and staring furiously at the world down below. 'They went after the pigeons and killed some of them. Betty and Spike and Clara. Set fire to them.'

There was a break in Skip's voice.

'Is he OK?' Mauve sounded shaken too.

'Aye,' said Skip. 'But Doo's old. He canny take that. I'll need to go over.'

He turned and punched the fence again. 'I should've gone and seen him when he'd no' written for a few days. It was her coming up here,' he glared at Kerrie, 'upsetting things, that's what stopped me going over to him like I always do. I should've been seeing to my old friends.'

Mauve stared very hard at her painting.

'I'm away over,' Skip said.

He scuffed over to the stairway.

Mauve made a face at Kerrie. 'He's upset.'

Kerrie forced a smile. 'Let's see what you've done to me,' she said, walking round to see her portrait.

Kerrie stared at the painting without interest. All at once she felt cut off from everything again, as if the bubble had sneaked up and silently slid over her, disconnecting her from the outside world.

Mauve fiddled about with her painting.

'I'm off to bed,' said Kerrie. She would maybe shake the thing off once safe inside her shed.

Mauve didn't turn, didn't even seem to hear Kerrie.

Her whole world was a patch of yellow in a corner of the canvas. Kerrie suddenly wanted to hurl the painting high over the rooftop fence, wanted to rip Mauve out of the safe, exclusive world she built around herself.

Instead she raced the bubble to the shed, shut the door against it, and curled so deep inside her sleeping bag she could hardly breathe.

It was the middle of the night when Kerrie woke, stiff with lying curled in the same position, sweating from the airless heat inside the sleeping bag. An unremembered dream still tugged at her and she went out on to the open roof to clear her head. It was a relief to have air on her face. There was no sign of the bubble. Thick above her, the stars burned with a hard, stabbing light.

In her mind Kerrie rehearsed how she would calmly refuse if the other two asked her to come busking in the morning. It really wasn't her scene, she'd say.

In the event, she sounded sharp and sore. It was only after they'd gone that Kerrie realized Skip hadn't even apologized. He'd just assumed she was still going. For a moment or two he'd stood bewildered, then walked quickly to the stairway door. Mauve hung around for a few moments but when Kerrie stuck her head in a book and ignored her, she left too.

Afterwards, Kerrie sat for a long while staring at nothing, ignoring the cold as it seeped up through the cement of the tower block and into her bones.

The sky had the first real look of autumn in it today,

a bare unmoving grey. Down below a bright red spot moved across the wide courtyard that connected the flats. A ladybird woman, laden with shopping bags. The only noise was the faraway hum of the city.

Kerrie looked around the empty rooftop. Shell wasn't due up till tomorrow and a long day stretched ahead. Suddenly she heard a flutter of wings and one of Doo's pigeons landed. It wandered over and waited until Kerrie untied the note from its foot.

LEAVE THE ROOF TODAY THE BIRDS SAY, read the note. THEY WILL KEEP WATCH.

How on earth could Doo's birds know what she was thinking? Kerrie wondered. She put out a saucer of bread and water for Restless, telling him Doo and the birds were just on the next roof. Then she pulled on her jacket and hat before she could change her mind. Getting caught couldn't be worse than this. Perhaps she wanted to get caught. Kerrie shivered, pulled her floppy hat close round her ears, and ran along the corridor to the lifts.

Skip had rattled at the locked door of her shed until Kerrie had finally yelled at him to buzz off and let her sleep. She looked at her clock. Nearly midnight. She'd come back up from the ground after ten, deliberately leaving it late until she was sure the other two would be back. Although she didn't want to see either of them, she couldn't face returning to an empty roof. And she rather liked the thought that they might be worrying about her.

Now he was playing that stupid tune on his mouth organ. Right outside her door. Well, fine. Kerrie pulled the quilt tight around her ears to block out the sound. Which it didn't. And now there was another noise, a scratching and a high whining. Kerrie sat up. 'Restless! Shut up, you stupid cat.' She threw a pillow at him, but Restless was engrossed in trying to scratch his way through the door to the noise.

Kerrie sighed and stared at her sunset picture, trying to draw some peace of mind from its wild dusk. When she finally gave in and opened the door there was relief, as if something in her muscles had unlocked.

'Hi,' growled the shadow.

Skip shuffled in and sat down on the bed. There was a lengthy silence.

'I feel just terrible.' He puffed out a sigh. 'Blasted me for ages, Mauve did.'

Kerrie looked at him for the first time since his outburst.

'Feel terrible about what?'

'What I said,' mumbled Skip.

'Oh?'

'I'm uh, you know.' He looked at her for help and got none.

'I don't,' said Kerrie.

'Sorry.'

He sounded miserable enough but she couldn't look at him.

'It wasny even true about Doo. I forgot about him. But I forget about him all the time till he sends me a

76

message. Mauve reminded me. I went up to see him today but he wasny there.'

Another sigh.

'Will you no' be a busker now?'

'I don't need your pity,' snapped Kerrie. She wouldn't tell him about her note from Doo. That was her secret.

'How no?'

'Because. I just thought – och, leave me alone.'

'You thought . . .' Skip screwed his face up to try to see what she would have thought. 'You're feeling bad,' he said at last.

'Oh, well done,' Kerrie muttered. 'I mean, I'm fine, just fine. I've decided I want to live on this roof like we're ordinary neighbours. We'll do our own thing and forget about trying to pretend we're all friendly.'

Skip stared at her unhappily. 'I didny know you were feeling that bad.'

He scooped up the kitten. 'Restless, what'll I do?' He stared into the kitten's luminous eyes for an answer then scrabbled in his pocket. 'You want my sparkly?'

'No.'

'I'll leave you it anyway,' he said.

He got up and stood staring at Kerrie's left foot. 'Where'd you go all day?' he asked.

'Down to the ground.'

'What'd you do?'

'Walked.' Kerrie found herself staring at the foot that Skip was fixed on, and nervously retied her boot-lace.

Skip nodded. 'It was OK then?'

Kerrie tutted. She had no intention of telling him.

She'd stood at a kerb, waiting for a break in an alarming rush of buses. The Wee Happy Bus passed on its way to the superstore, smudges of weary faces just visible through the grime on its windows. Two men pushed a sofa, with a toddler bouncing delightedly on its cushions, down the steep hill from the flats. Kerrie had watched it all like a visitor from another world.

Then she found herself walking the familiar route to school. She heard the clamour of voices before she turned the corner and knew it was breaktime. Kerrie hesitated then walked up to the fence, scanning the crowded playground. Shell was sitting on the grass with Janis and some other girls, within calling distance. Kerrie pressed her face between two railings.

'Shell,' she hissed. Of course Shell wouldn't hear that. She'd have to shout.

'What you looking at, tinker?' a boy called over. He stuffed his hands in his pockets and strode over to the fence. Kerrie drew back.

'What do you want, tink?'

The boy almost spat out the words.

'Shell.' Kerrie nodded towards the group of girls. 'She's my pal.'

The boy raised his eyebrows. He glanced at Shell, then looked Kerrie up and down.

'Shell McCormack,' he yelled suddenly. 'This dirty wee tink's telling me she's your pal.'

Kerrie felt faces turn to look at her. She turned and ran.

It had started to rain in hard lines. She took shelter under the canopy of the grocery store and stared out at wet grey and the occasional orange splash of a passing bus.

Something slithered and moaned at her elbow, and she jumped. A baby in a pushchair, covered in a plastic rainsheet, twisted round to look at her from inside its capsule and let out a grin. Kerrie laughed at herself. She walked out into the rain, taking the road that led out of the housing scheme.

Away from the streets and the city, the buildings flattened into sky and field. She walked for miles, as far as the little man-made loch with its new trees and smooth green meadows that she and Gran used to take the bus out to on fine Sundays. She sat on a bench and dried out a bit in weak bursts of sun.

An elderly woman on a nearby bench was writing a letter, smiling to herself as she read over bits of it. Kerrie chewed her knuckle as the idea came to her. She went over to the woman and asked if she could buy a piece of paper and an envelope from her. The woman looked up, surprised. As she took in Kerrie's grubby appearance, she pulled her handbag closer.

'Forget it,' muttered Kerrie, and went back over to her bench. A moment later the woman approached, and held out a stamped envelope.

'Sorry, hen. I just got a fright, you appearing in front of me like that. My son says I shouldn't sit out by myself in the park just in case. It's peaceful though.' She turned to go.

'You'll not have a pen, eh?' She was back, handing Kerrie a Biro.

'Ta.' Kerrie smiled at her. 'I probably look like a mugger in this state.'

The woman hesitated. 'Are you all right, dear?'

Kerrie could see that the woman wanted her to say yes, she was fine.

'No problem,' Kerrie smiled. 'I'll bring your Biro over in a minute.'

'No, you keep it. I've got plenty at home.'

The woman was fiddling in her handbag. She put something in Kerrie's hand. 'They just clutter up my purse, hen,' she said and hurried away.

Kerrie looked at the pound coin in her hand. Inside the envelope were two pieces of folded writing paper. Nice wee woman. She twiddled the pen in her fingers. How to write it all down in just two pages? What did she want to say anyway? Dear Mum, sorry for running away when you needed me most, I want to take up your offer and come home now. Just so you don't drive me up the wall this time round, here are some ground rules . . . or Dear Mum, I'd just like to send you a wee note to tell you how I've felt all these years . . . I'm making my own life now so you don't have to worry.

I'll just have to write and see what comes out, Kerrie decided.

A darkening of the green and a ripple on the water finally made her look up. The watery sunlight had deepened, turning the edges of the heavy clouds copper. Kerrie realized she'd been writing for ages; she was cold to the bone. She folded the letter, put it in the envelope, and shoved it in her back pocket, and began the long walk home.

Now, back in her shed with Skip shuffling about, something in the cold that had seeped deeper and deeper into her all day seemed to have withered all her feelings. Kerrie let the silence spread between her and Skip. He probably wouldn't have understood.

Skip let out a wrenching sigh. He hesitated then said, 'You keep it. As long as you want. It's my best thing,' he said, as if she didn't know, and left.

Kerrie stared at the sparkly he'd placed on the floor by her feet, its colours gently disturbed by the candle-light. Her cold legs wouldn't move at first, then she had to dodge Restless to get out the door. The rooftop was a black, alien place after the candlelit shed.

'Skip, wait a minute.'

Kerrie crashed into the oil-drums that she'd rolled into a neat group in the centre of the rooftop and came to a halt, rubbing a bruised kneecap. The bulky shadow of his coat was in front of her.

'That was daft,' he said.

She heard the scrape of a match and a soft cloud of light enclosed them. Kerrie couldn't think of what it was she wanted to say.

It came in a gabbled rush. 'You really want to be friends or d'you just feel sorry for me?'

'Daft question as well,' he said. 'I wouldny leave you my sparkly, now would I?'

'D'you – d'you want Restless then?'

'For keeps?' Skip asked.

'He might no' understand.'

But Skip was grinning, shaking his head. He paused a moment to discard the flame that was nibbling at his fingers and lit a new one.

'Mauve sold my painting the day. She's finishing yours then we're off for another busk. The three of us.'

It was almost a question.

Kerrie closed her mind to doubts.

'I'll come and watch.'

Skip nodded and the cloud of light died. Kerrie turned and clattered into another oil-drum.

Crazy like the
moon

A middle-aged man and woman were dithering about the display of paintings Mauve had set up on the pavement between two shop doorways. This spot in the city centre pedestrian precinct was Mauve's favourite in the mornings because, she explained, the light was just right. And there was space in front for Skip to busk.

Another shopper paused to watch Skip's performance, her eyes wandering to Mauve's arresting backdrop scenes. Her other-worldly paintings matched his offbeat music perfectly, thought Kerrie. It was no wonder people stopped in their separate tracks to have a look. Their tight, busied expressions would loosen as curiosity and amusement at Mauve and Skip's strange spectacle gathered them in with the rest of the small crowd.

Kerrie had nudged Mauve, who was busy sketching, to draw her attention to the middle-aged couple who, she thought, looked as if they were dressed for a day in a muddy field. They had begun to squabble about the painting that featured herself. Kerrie listened in, but they were talking jargon, all concepts and archetypes and she soon lost interest. She couldn't see that any of it had much to do with the painting. It was so deeply alive; their talk was flat, blank, a cheap gleam on their fancy words.

Skip's boot poked her. He was bothering her about tuning up, which she'd no intention of doing. She'd had no intention of bringing her guitar along with her either but Skip had nipped back up to the roof on a pretext while she and Mauve walked to the bus stop, and he'd arrived with it slung over his shoulder.

'You'll maybe fancy a wee turn once you're there,' he'd smirked.

Now, huddled against a wall in the bustle of the pedestrian precinct, with that ever-changing audience of shoppers, Kerrie felt even less inclined. Her hat pulled well down, she sneaked glimpses at the ring of faces, dreading a familiar one. But all the eyes were on Skip. In front of an audience he had suddenly assumed an alien personality and stood jerking in time to his music, breathing energy from his mouth organ.

All of yesterday's loneliness had passed. These days, Kerrie was constantly surprised by her mind's ability to shove away unhappy thoughts. She saw a cupboard in her head stuffed with all her bad memories and wondered if she should ever try to open it. Have a clearing-out day for old clutter like Gran used to. Maybe not. The likelihood was that a pile of stuff would come spewing out, like the jumper shelf in her wardrobe at home – she used to think a little demon must live in there, waiting to kick out all her jumpers whenever she opened the door. If she opened her memory cupboard it might take ages, with a little demon struggling against her, to sort it all out. Better leave things where they were.

Skip was rocking from side to side now in time to a jigging tune that was vaguely familiar. Coins clattered in the hamburger box he had retrieved from a litter bin and placed a little in front of his feet.

'Just give me some background. On you go. You know this one.' Skip was whining at her, poking her leg with his toe. Out of embarrassment Kerrie took up her guitar, strummed a vague chord or two, and felt the gaze of the crowd harden on her. She could feel Skip grinning in victory, the slug. He'd planned this all along.

'That's her there.'

Kerrie started in fright at the words then realized it was only Mauve talking to the couple in wellingtons, waving her over. The couple seemed to have reached a calmer point in their discussions but Mauve looked like she could do with some help. Kerrie took her chance to escape.

'I do like this theme of street urchins as aliens in fantasy city-scapes. It's vibrantly done, it makes its point.'

The woman tucked a strand of smooth, grey-blonde hair behind her ear and glanced through Kerrie.

Mauve looked uncomfortable.

The man frowned. 'Out of place, out of time, out on a limb. Well, it's topical enough. Will it sell though?'

The woman answered with an impatient flap of her hand. The man looked defeated as she took out her wallet.

Kerrie's heart sank at the thought of losing her painting to strangers, especially such grey and squabbly ones. This morning, when she'd seen it finished, she knew just how Skip had felt about his sparkly portrait. There was a disturbing power in Mauve's paintings, as if something uncanny was on the verge of happening. She captured the essence of your own self and merged it with a magical, other dimension. And what that couple had said – she hadn't seen that before but it was true. The three of them were like aliens living out on a limb on their rooftop.

Kerrie stared at her image for the last time. Shrapnel, Mauve called it. In it, she wore nondescript, timeless clothing; there was a sheen like metal from it in the light of a brilliant, sun-reflected sky. The windows of the tower blocks blazed around her like regiments of shields, the vast shadow of invisible wings touching them. Beyond, the city lay dull as ash, a dead thing in the dusk. Her eyes in the painting reflected the sea-green of the stones set in her earrings, and of a stone that she looked set to throw out of the painting, right at the onlooker, it seemed.

Green was the colour of magic, it held a power, Mauve said, being the colour of nature. The soft sparks of it splintered the harder bronze of the sun, the sky, glass and metal. Kerrie wasn't sure what the battle was, but something in the image both excited and repelled her.

The woman was saying something else to Mauve, who flushed red and looked dazed. She took out her cheque book as Mauve began to wrap her paintings in old newspaper. Mauve piled them all in a small stack, then placed the one of Kerrie, unwrapped, on top.

'Careful,' she warned the woman. 'That one's still a bit wet.'

As the couple struggled off with their horde, Kerrie watched the image of her own face disappear.

'Well?' demanded Skip who had curtailed his performance.

'The lot in one go,' breathed Mauve. 'They own a wee art gallery, she said, and they want to show them there and sell them.'

'Aye, but did she pay you?' asked Skip warily. 'Remember that con man you fell for the last time.'

Mauve's face dropped.

'But she gave me a cheque and her business card. I've to see them tomorrow at her gallery. She wants to "talk possibilities".'

Skip examined the cheque. He flapped it in Mauve's face.

'Will you look at this? For a load of paintings? You sure?'

Mauve and Kerrie crowded him to look.

'Canny be.'

Mauve had gone all breathless again.

87

'It is. It must be,' said Kerrie, scrutinizing the cheque. 'You could live off this for months.'

'Ya beauty,' Skip whispered, looking as shaken as Mauve. Then he recovered himself. 'Right then. First, we find us a bank, and second,' he sighed, 'It's a long time since I've been in a Pizza Hut.'

The bank teller had taken an agonizingly slow time to look over Mauve's stock of identification: a couple of letters from her social security office, a library card and her passport. She looked up and smiled insincerely from time to time at the bedraggled bunch clogging up her bit of the counter.

'Where've you been?' asked Kerrie, as the teller handed Mauve back her passport.

'Nowhere yet,' Mauve slid a reflection of the teller's smile back across the counter as the woman queried her lack of a bank account and the irregularity of an uncrossed cheque.

'Which means I don't need a bank account, right? And that's definitely me in the passport, right? So there's no problem, right?'

The teller got up to whisper with somebody behind a screen. Skip elbowed Kerrie.

'Impressive, eh? She can be right on the ball when she puts her mind to it.' He laughed, a chuffing sound like a steam train in a tunnel.

Outside, Mauve deposited wads of notes in various places around her person – in pockets and socks, secured by a rubber band to her wrist, in her paintbox.

'What do we need?' she asked.

'Need?' said Kerrie.

'Like – socks and toothbrushes, knickers, a pile of chewing gum, oh, and I want new brushes and paints.' Mauve was skipping backwards down the street, bumping into somebody at every second step, the bag full of all her bits and pieces clanking on her back.

Skip shuffled after her, adding to her list. 'Some of those wee soft face wipes you get in Boots, for skin as soft as a baby's bum. I love them.'

Kerrie caught their bug. 'Oh, I've been in agony for a Marks & Spencer toffee pudding, and cheesy muffins.'

Giggling, her guitar bumping off her back, Kerrie ran after the other two. And as she ran she remembered Saturdays when she'd race Shell and Janis and Sarah through crowds of shoppers, pocket money from Gran crumpled in her pocket. They'd hit Boots with the force of four small tornadoes, where they'd all argue over whether to buy peach- or toffee-flavoured lipsalve. They'd squirt perfume at each other and draw stars and crescent moons on their cheeks with silver eye-pencils until a painted-doll assistant threatened them with a security guard.

Kerrie slowed to a walk. It was only last month yet it seemed worlds away. She swallowed the lump in her throat. That's gone, she told herself. So let it go.

Mauve would get her some peach lipsalve.

*

'You bored, pal, just standing all day?' Skip asked a pale-faced security guard who had started to follow them round Marks & Spencer's food hall. 'You have a wee wander with us then, if it'll pass the time for you.'

'Shoosh,' murmured Kerrie. 'We'll get chucked out.'

'Nope, Mauve's rich now, we won't. And I've got my sparkly, remember.'

'So?'

'Special protection,' winked Skip.

'Rubbish,' said Kerrie.

'Think so? Watch this, then.' Skip nipped round past the bread counter, slipping out of sight of the security guard. He took a packet of chocolate chip cookies from a shelf, stuffed them inside his coat and walked off, his sparkly held out in front of him like a tiny shield.

'Total loony,' Kerrie muttered to herself. 'Oh, now he's done it.'

A security bleeper had gone off. Kerrie hurried to the checkouts. The stupid, stupid . . .

But there Skip was, grinning, halfway up the escalator. The security guard was shaking his finger at one of the sales assistants, kidding her on. 'Sick of you lot of incompetents setting off my alarms,' he was shouting across at her. The young woman laughed, her face pink with embarrassment. Kerrie ran up the escalator.

'See?' said Skip.

'Don't be so daft. That assistant set off his bleeper and he didn't see you. Lucky for you.'

'Exactly,' said Skip. 'Always works. Now where's that Mauve got to?'

'Are you telling me you really believe that was your sparkly?' asked Kerrie, as they scanned the street outside for Mauve.

'I told you. It's my special protection, never fails. It's got magic powers.'

Kerrie shook her head. He was a lost cause.

Skip was staring at her, that annoying smirk on his face.

'What?' demanded Kerrie.

He lunged in her jacket pocket. Kerrie struggled but he held out Gran's folded-up sweetie paper, her tiny emerald jewel.

'What's this then?'

'Give it, Skip. Give!'

He danced around her.

'What you carrying this around for then? It's your lucky thing, I've seen you.'

He looked at it closer. 'It's just a folded-up sweetie paper. You really believe this'll keep you safe, then?'

'It's my gran's.'

Skip stopped dancing about like an idiot. Kerrie wanted to hit him. If he was nice to her now she'd hit him, hard.

Skip shoved the tiny parcel back in her pocket, drew inside his coat and shuffled off.

'C'mon. Mauve's away wandering and she's got all the goodies,' he called over his shoulder.

Kerrie stood for a moment, feeling furious, then

stupid. She had to admit she did hang on to the sweetie paper like it was her talisman. But at least she didn't believe it made her invisible. Still, it made her almost as daft as Skip, didn't it? He had his sparkly, she had her green jewel, like the green gemstone she held in her hand in Mauve's painting. Kerrie realized that Mauve must know about the sweetie paper too. Only she'd painted it as a green gemstone.

Skip had found Mauve round the corner, weighed down with plastic bags, her nose flat against the window of the Gallery of New Scottish Art.

'Nothing very new in all that,' she tutted. 'I mean, a couple of mountains and trees, a loch and a purply sky, painted all slapdash. Now I could really do something different with that.'

'So you could,' Skip nodded. 'You'd have a spaceship in disguise as a giant packet of cheese 'n' onion crisps zooming over a big mountain, causing a sheep stampede, and a gang of metal-skinned aliens splashing themselves into rust in a Highland stream. Did you know Mauve used to paint supermarket queues, Kerrie?'

'Supermarket queues?'

'Aye, that's how she started,' Skip continued. 'She'd sit on one of the wee benches you get near the checkouts and paint all the people and the food coming through in a big blur. She's a one-off, our Mauve.'

Kerrie nodded. You couldn't disagree. The image of that blur of colour Skip had just described sprang at her. She'd seen it somewhere, and then she remembered. It had been hanging in the kitchen at Ruth's, Mauve's friend in the flats. She'd noticed it one night Mauve had sneaked her down for a bath.

'What'll we do now?' asked Mauve. 'I don't feel like going back yet.'

They looked around the street, busy now with the exodus of office workers.

'It says here, "Buzzy Wares isn't just open till midnight, it's wide awake,"' Skip read off a board attached to a lamp-post. 'Buzzy Wares – I wish I was called that. That's the best name I ever heard. You can call me that from now on. Buzz for short.'

'I kinda like October Bistro.' Kerrie pulled her velvet hat around her face Bo-Peep style. 'Hi, I'm October, October Bistro.'

Skip giggled and stepped back into a figure. 'Whoops, awfy sorry.'

'Buy the *Big Issue* magazine. Help the homeless help themselves,' the figure suddenly droned, as if Skip's bump had activated a voice-start button. You could only see the seller's nose, the collar of his donkey jacket was pulled so high over his chin, and a cap was hard down over his eyes.

'Sure, pal,' said Skip. 'Mauve, you got money for that guy? Help us to help ourselves, like he says.'

Mauve purchased a copy from the donkey jacket and thwacked Skip with it.

'We'd better find him a Pizza Hut,' she said to Kerrie, 'or else he's so high he's gonny burst.'

*

'If I died the night I'd die truly happy,' said Skip much later, as they spilled out of the fuggy warmth of the pizzeria into damp night air.

Mauve crunched peppermints. She'd crammed handfuls into her pockets as she waited for change. Kerrie unzipped her guitar case and flourished a collection of small packets of sugar, salt and assorted sauces. Skip looked unimpressed and opened his coat to reveal a large plastic menu clamped under his arm.

'Oh yum,' said Kerrie. 'Very tasty. What're we supposed to do with that, dummy? Torment ourselves to death one night over a Pot Noodle?'

'I've got an imagination,' Skip retorted. 'I can sit and look at it and kid myself when I'm skint and miserable.'

'Bundle of fun, that.'

But Skip was placid from eating an entire sixteen-inch prawn pizza. He threw an arm over Mauve's shoulder and hugged her.

'Brilliant,' he said.

Kerrie fell behind them, exhausted by what she'd just eaten. It had been long weeks since she'd had a proper meal. Food was no longer something to be gorged or discarded on a whim, it was a resource to be rationed and chewed slowly, even the bits you would normally have left for the bin, like peas and rubbery cheese. Tonight had felt like the rediscovery of a lost sense.

The other two had sparked themselves into another daft mood, and were chasing each other in and out of car headlamps. Crazy like the moon – Gran used to say that about her and Shell. Many moons ago, it seemed now.

As they'd munched through their pizzas, Skip had cast up all sorts of plans for Mauve's windfall, and in each one he'd assumed Kerrie would be there. And so she'd felt herself unwinding, more relaxed than she had been since Gran died, and had sat back cocooned in their frantic chatter, eating her fill.

She'd have to hurry to keep up now or she'd lose them. Kerrie ran through what seemed like currents of tension. It was in voices and faces, in the push of people, in the gaps where they avoided touching: tension was the very energy of the city. She thought of the rooftop, distant and safe under the gentle hum of the stars; you couldn't hear it but you almost felt it on your eardrums, in the bones of your head. You could, as Mauve said, be whatever you wanted up there. But down here in the streets you were part of a great mechanism, cramped under a dome of taut energy, pressed along with everyone else into the pattern of the city.

On the roof there was no pattern, thought Kerrie. There was only sky and wide open space, day and night, and the faraway drone of another world.

They took a taxi home, the plastic bags from their shopping spree tumbling all over the floor.

'A magic day, eh?' said Skip. 'The most magic one since . . .' He thought back as the taxi rumbled up the hill to the tower blocks.

Kerrie felt the charge of excitement around the flats the instant she stepped out of the taxi. Before she could gather her thoughts Skip was yelling, pushing her aside to get out of the door. At the foot of their tower block was a fleet of great gleaming machines. Kerrie was aware of flashing lights, darting fluorescent uniforms and a cacophony of shouts, sirens and barking dogs. She felt Mauve at her side, gripping her like she was a lifebuoy or an anchor, as they walked into the storm of confusion and noise.

Skip had vanished. He'd raced ahead and Kerrie had lost sight of him in the crowd that was gathered in the courtyard between the flats. He wouldn't try to go up there, surely. They wouldn't let him.

She turned to Mauve whose face was sharp, ghostly in the lights, her eyes wide and terrified.

'It's Doo's roof as well,' said Mauve. 'Both of them are on fire.' Her voice sounded cracked as if she had fought through the filthy, pouring smoke and the flames that lit up the two rooftops like beacons.

Kerrie turned cold all over. Doo's note from yesterday. What had it said? *Leave the roof today the birds say*. Oh, how could she have been so stupid, so self-centred? The note hadn't been about her. Doo's birds must have told him there was trouble coming to the rooftops. It was a warning to all of them. But didn't that mean Doo would be safe, that he would have left the roof?

'Mauve,' called Kerrie, but Mauve was racing through the fire engines, ignoring the shouts of police officers to keep back. Kerrie ran after her to where Skip was pinned against a police van, yelling at the two officers who were restraining him. He saw Mauve.

'Tell them, Mauve, tell them about Doo. They'll no' listen.'

'I'm listening, son, and if anybody's alive up there they'll be found. Now cool it down or I'm locking you in the van.' The officer handed Skip over to Mauve. 'Better look after him.'

Fright stretched Skip's face. He had shrunk inside his huge coat.

Mauve pushed him over to the grass at the far edge of the courtyard, away from the blazing lights, and made him sit down. Kerrie sat on the other side of him and linked her arm through his.

'He sent a note, Skip, to warn us,' Kerrie said. 'He knew something, the birds told him. I should have told you. Maybe he got off the roof. Maybe he's OK.'

Skip took the sparkly from his pocket. He cupped it in his hands and gazed into it. 'Come on, Doo,' he whispered, wiping away his breath-mist with a sleeve as if he believed that might dull its power to keep Doo safe.

Kerrie watched the fires feeding on the rooftops. They spat out chunks of debris that hurtled down the sides of the buildings like bits of falling star. It was an awful image of unfettered energy.

But it's beautiful, thought Kerrie. Terrible and beautiful. You must be able to see it for miles and miles. People in planes'll wonder what it is. There'll be someone on a rooftop at the other side of the city watching it, thinking how lovely it looks. Great fire torches in the night.

And then she remembered: Restless was on the roof.

When Shell finally found her, Kerrie was calm. Shell was loud and hysterical, hugging her. Kerrie pushed her away.

'We thought you were dead,' said Shell.

Kerrie shrugged and lay on the grass verge staring up at the low, sulphurous sky.

'Come home with me tonight and my mum'll sort it all out. She will. It's best, Kerrie.'

Kerrie dug her nails in the grass. A feeling had been growing these last few weeks that she had ignored, hadn't wanted to examine – the feeling that she was moving beyond Shell and the others. And Shell couldn't see it. Or she did and kept trying to drag Kerrie back to where they were before, which was impossible. Kerrie knew she had flung herself too far outside of ordinary life to go back now; she was being dragged further and further out each day by an invisible tide. And tonight that tide had left her stranded on a tiny island with just Skip and Mauve to cling to.

Shell was still pleading with her.

'It's gone too far. Something's going to happen to you and it'll be my fault. I made you do it.'

'Shell, I'm staying with Skip and Mauve. I'm like them now.'

'You're nothing like them, they're just a couple of – of wasters. Anyway, you've nowhere to go now. Kerrie, this is crazy. Come home with me and we'll get something sorted.'

Kerrie shook her head and switched off from Shell.

'If you can get out of it go. Your pal's right. It's crazy, the whole world's crazy. Go.' Skip was glowering down at her like he used to, like she was a stranger again.

Kerrie sat up and glared back at him.

'It's as crazy inside as out,' she snapped.

'Kerrie, please,' whispered Shell.

'Everything's different. I'm sorry, Shell.'

'Go for it,' said a raw voice behind her. 'I would.'

It was Sarah. Kerrie met Sarah's eyes as she yanked Shell to her feet and pulled her away. Kerrie watched them disappear in the crowd.

Sarah, thought Kerrie, I should have tried to reach you.

'You're crazy,' Skip muttered beside her.

Kerrie dug her heel into the spongy grass.

'Yeah. Like the moon.'

Black alley, tinder morning

The homeless hostel in a nearby church hall was full, packed early due to the chill of autumn in the night air. Kerrie glimpsed a floor scattered with mattresses and litter, huddles of people, the air fugged with cigarettes and paraffin fumes. She drew in deep breaths of frost-sharp air as she walked down the hill with Mauve, Skip dragging behind them, to the community centre. Any amount of cold was better than that awful hostel.

Mauve found her friend, Ruth, at the community centre, huddled inside a sleeping bag with her baby, and white with worry. Ruth had struggled down the flights of stairs with baby Kate, imagining Mauve cremated on the rooftop.

Even if there hadn't been the risk of someone recognizing Kerrie, Mauve said, the centre was full to bursting with evacuees from the tower blocks.

Skip didn't seem to care what was happening and cowered into his coat, a snail inside his shell, silent and shivering.

For several long hours they had waited. Eventually

Mauve had gone over to one of the fire-officers and came back defeated, dodging Skip's eyes.

'They've no' found him,' he said, sounding as if he'd been shaken from a deep sleep.

'No,' admitted Mauve.

In the pumpkin glow of the streetlamps Skip's face lit up ghoulishly.

'Kerrie says he sent a note, he knew there was trouble coming. He'll have gone home then. He wouldny even be up there.'

Skip set off down the hill to the bus stop. Kerrie nudged Mauve who was staring up at the flats.

'Come on. He's not fit to be on his own.'

She was remembering that first night after Gran's death and her own unfocused, dangerous frame of mind.

Doo's sometime home was an attic flat, deep in the city, at the back of a run of short alleyways. The stone stairs of the close dipped with the wear of generations of footsteps. A sluggish smell of chip fat hung dead in the air. At the top of the stairs Skip held his thumb over the doorbell. He didn't press it.

'D'you think he's here?' He stared hard at the door.

Mauve sighed.

Skip pressed the bell.

Some of the stairlights were out and in the murk the figure at the door was just a shadow. Kerrie had an impression of hair curling round thin shoulders, of a fragile figure.

Skip stuttered out his question.

101

'No, sorry, son. He sometimes comes on a Sunday for his tea, but I've not seen him for a while now. That's his way, you know.'

There was a silence as they all stood stupidly in the dark, then Kerrie heard her head crack against the stone wall as Skip slammed past her down the stairs. As Mauve began to speak to the woman, Kerrie felt a rise of panic and struggled down through the dark of the close, her guitar banging against her back.

The orange of the streetlamps dazzled her like sunlight for a moment but she glimpsed Skip disappearing down one of the alleyways. Kerrie thought fleetingly of Mauve, then she was racing after him into the unlit alley, tripping over rough ground, negotiating unidentifiable obstacles and fighting to find enough breath to yell at him to stop.

A great, black obstacle moved from the shadows and broke her run, twisting her arm in his grip.

Skip said something she didn't hear, her pulse was hammering so hard in her head. His voice was as cold as stone though.

'I know I should have told you about his note. I was angry,' Kerrie burst out.

Skip turned away, shaking his head, walking further into the dark.

'I'm getting out of it,' he muttered over his shoulder.

The thought of Skip alone in these black alleys made Kerrie follow him.

'You'll just go off and do something daft,' she muttered and grabbed a bit of his coat. Skip pulled his coat about him, trying to shake her off. Then he gave up.

'I'm feeling crazy,' he said. 'I canny see a way of getting myself through the night. I'm having such crazy thoughts about the world. I hate it.'

'Like I've been feeling all these weeks. But I managed. I got through.'

Surprised, Kerrie realized that she had.

'Maybe you wanted to. Maybe I don't, see? No' any more. Maybe you're stronger than me. Or no' as stupid.'

'Stupider,' said Kerrie.

At the far end of the lightless alleyway a motorbike revved, stirring up some dogs. Skip rubbed his hands over his face like he did in the morning when he stumbled out of his shed into daylight.

'Who says you've got to live like this?' he demanded. 'Somebody else did 'cause I never decided to be like this. Things just happened to me.'

'I know. Things happen so you do what you can.'

'That's it,' nodded Skip.

Kerrie shivered with relief now that Skip was beginning to talk, however morbidly. As long as he talked, she could hang on to him. She began to edge him back towards the main road.

'Poor lady,' said Skip, looking up to the attic window. 'But she'll maybe think he just stayed with his pigeons. She's better off thinking that.'

'Why didn't he live with his wife?' asked Kerrie.

'His sister. He never married. Prefers birds to people.

He used to live in the country when he was a boy. Away up near the mountains. He learned all about the birds there. He hated the city and then one day he found the rooftop and his pigeons. He loves them. They go to her too. Up there, all round her wee attic window.'

Skip frowned.

'I'm talking like he's still here. D'you think he's alive? D'you no' think I'd know if he was dead?'

Kerrie thought of the morning Gran died. Hadn't she known there was something wrong? No, she'd been too wrapped up in herself and the band.

She scanned the street. 'We'll need to find Mauve.'

'Oh, she'll have gone away back to the centre. She usually gives up on me when I get crazy,' said Skip.

'So what'll we do?'

'Find a bed.'

Skip was heading back down the alleyway, steadily this time, looking all about him.

'Find a bed here?' said Kerrie.

'There'll be something. Always is.'

Kerrie sighed. He seemed to know what he was looking for. They crossed into an adjoining alleyway, a less daunting one lit by several bent streetlamps. Along both sides was a series of rickety huts, crammed together and so small and higgledy-piggledy they had a gnome-like look about them. Warm smells of garlic, hot bread and tomato, sounds of clattering pots and pans and the buzz of chatter came from further down the alleyway.

'Aha,' said Skip.

He was peering through windows with a match, pushing against doors. One hut, its roof so lopsided it had a drunken appearance, needed only a kick or two before its door collapsed.

'Perfect.' Skip showed Kerrie the interior with his tiny flame.

'Well, absolutely. Hotel standard.'

The floor was littered with paint tins and scraps of wood. Its single piece of furniture was a workbench, with a selection of tools neatly arranged on the wall above it, all thick with dust.

'Now,' he said.

'Don't tell me. That stinky old mattress over there under the streetlight.'

'Well spotted. It's the very thing,' said Skip, kicking the worst of the grime out of it. They dragged the mattress into the hut. There was barely enough room. An ancient dustsheet served as a blanket.

'Roll yourself up in it,' advised Skip. 'And leave me some.'

The practical demands of organizing shelter for the night seemed to have pushed away his nightmare, at least for the present.

'That smell,' groaned Kerrie as they settled themselves on the mattress. 'Garlic bread, and I'm starving. Listen to my stomach.'

'You'd never believe that was just tonight, eh?' yawned Skip.

Kerrie stared up into the dark. Tonight at the pizzeria. It seemed like another life. And busking in the precinct. It was just like that endless, timeless day when Gran died. What time was it? She held up her wrist to catch the light of the streetlamp through the tiny window. Just after one. Strange how time could stretch itself like that and cram so much life into one day.

Already, Skip had sunk into the deep breathing of an exhausted sleep. Kerrie lay wide awake, turning her green gem over and over in her fingers. The night's events had left her buzzing. She tried to calm herself with thoughts of all the sure and steady things she could still trust. Her guitar, that was something. Skip and Mauve. Well, that was about all. Outside the hut a cat cried like a baby and Kerrie screwed up her face as she remembered she didn't have Restless any more. She turned over for the umpteenth time, jostling Skip who erupted in a gabble of sleep talk.

Carefully, Kerrie unwound herself from the dustsheet and crept out into the alleyway. The streetlamps cowered, lights quivering against the dark backdrop of tenement buildings. There was a precarious feel to the rows of crooked little huts, as if the vibrations of the clattering restaurant and the thrumming city might demolish them. And the sky, bloated with low clouds that reflected the orange of the streetlamps, was too vivid for a night sky. Every so often the clouds flung themselves apart to reveal the stark, horrified face of the moon.

Kerrie went back inside the hut and curled up close to Skip. Sleep like his only happened when you didn't care much if you lived or died. It was like falling into the blackness at the edge of the roof and landing up somewhere safe and warm. Kerrie had known sleep like that the first week on the roof. She wouldn't sleep like that tonight.

Kerrie leaned over and watched Skip's face, framed in a lozenge of orange lamplight, his hard-set features softened by the glow and the depth of his sleep. There was movement behind his eyelids, gentle as the slither of a snail, a catch in his breathing. He might be in trouble. You never wake someone out of a dream, Kerrie knew that, but she didn't know why. There must be some danger in wrenching someone out of the depths of their own mind, just as a diver gets the bends if hauled too rapidly to the surface.

Maybe, if she talked of something hopeful in the real world, it would get through. That was a point. Kerrie cast about for something. A patch of clear, starry sky in the corner of the hut's small window caught her eye and suddenly she remembered Grandpa's star.

'That star,' Gran would tell her, pointing out a bright star set in a group of duller ones, 'that's your grandpa's star.' The star had winked at her the night after he died and right away Gran knew that was him. Sounds daft, but she just knew. That was where he'd gone, a million miles away. But he could still wink at her like he always did and kid her on.

Gran would have her own star now and so would Doo, Kerrie whispered. Skip would just have to hold on for a clear night until they could find them.

*

Late next morning Skip and Kerrie found Mauve sitting on the steps at the community centre. Mauve was in a scalding temper but they both held their tongues and by the time they were out on the street she was chattering away about some holiday she was taking them on.

Skip looked at her in disbelief.

'A holiday? Have you cracked up, girl? I was just kidding you on about all that.'

'Listen,' said Mauve. 'I've had an idea. I've been up all night thinking about it. I went to see that woman at the gallery first thing this morning. I've got all this money and it looks like there'll be more when I get back. After last night I've decided I want a way out of the city. Sheila, that's the gallery woman, she's interested in a new set of paintings . . . see, I want to keep using your faces but in different landscapes, with different ideas. Archie, that's her partner, said you gave the pictures complexity.'

'Did he? Aye, I thought he looked intelligent,' said Skip. 'But seriously, Mauve, we canny use up your money. It wouldny solve anything. No' in the long run.'

'Och, rubbish,' said Mauve.

But Skip wasn't listening any more. He was studying the haze of smoke that hung around the rooftops of the tower blocks.

'Listen,' he said. 'I need to go and see if I can find any of Doo's birds.'

Kerrie nodded. This morning she and Skip had emerged from the alleyway hut coughing and sneezing, with a taste of garlic and dust in their mouths. The tearing sound of wings had made her look up. Loose clouds and leaves blew about the sky and a pigeon flew to join a flock that clamoured around a tiny arch-shaped window set in the roof of the tenement flats on the main road. Kerrie had pointed them out to Skip, who dragged his eyes from the ground where he'd been kicking up litter and tindery drifts of leaves.

'Maybe they're Doo's,' she'd suggested. 'Maybe they know to go to his sister now.'

Skip had been calmer then, and had watched the sky all the way back on the bus.

Even if they could get back up to the roof now, Kerrie wasn't sure if she'd want to. Their world had been violated; it would never feel the same again.

Skip was taking ages, and Kerrie was getting increasingly twitchy in case someone she knew passed by. Then he appeared from behind Doo's tower block. For someone who had been suicidal the previous night, Skip now appeared incredibly buoyant, Kerrie observed, as he bounded over the courtyard, his coat flapping behind him like great wings.

He was yelling ecstatically.

'I've found him,' he was shouting. And then, as he reached them, his face crumpled as if he was in pain. He turned his back to them. He was shaking so much Kerrie could see the shivers through the thickness of his huge coat.

'You mean Doo?' whispered Mauve. 'He's alive?'

The back of Skip's head jerked in a nod. For a while

he did nothing but sniff, then he turned round and began to tell them how he'd tried to get up on to Doo's roof but the top flight of stairs had been blocked off by the fire crews. As he'd run down the flights and flights of stairs, stopping for breath on the landings, he'd looked out over the patch of wasteland that was to one side of the tower blocks and seen a flutter of birds. He'd looked closer and his heart had thudded so hard it hurt when he saw Doo's red knitted hat bobbing in among them.

He'd run across, shouting at such a pitch with the breath he had left that he'd scared all the birds away.

'See, he thought we'd got his note and gone and he was watching out from the ground all the time. He'd taken the birds down with him. They're all OK.'

He'd told Doo about Mauve's plan to go up north.

'I told him to come. It's where he's from. But he says he's going back to his sister, they're both too old to be on their own now and she won't move. I never thought he was old before but today he looked like an old man, his face was all fallen to pieces.' Skip sniffed again, and shook his head. 'But he's alive. I knew if I believed hard enough the sparkly'd keep him safe.'

'You've decided you're coming then,' Mauve said drily.

Skip didn't hear her. He had grabbed Kerrie's arm. 'We're going up North. Mauve's gonny paint us in the mountains – mountains and lochs, all that stuff,' he gabbled. 'I canny believe it.'

He looked up behind him, his face suddenly tight as the night's events came back to him.

'All that stuff Doo talks about. He sends his birds there. He says he can smell the pine and the fern and the peat off them. And now I'm gonny see it. He says it's meant. There's always good comes out of bad, he says.'

Skip shook his head again and swallowed.

'It'll be a new start,' said Mauve. 'A wide-open new world.'

'But it means using up your money, Mauve,' said Kerrie. She was torn between wanting to go, and feeling that events were spiralling out of control again. But there was nothing for her here now.

'You'll be earning it. You're my models. I need your faces. Anyway, where'll you go if you stay here?'

Skip was doing what looked like a rain dance beside her.

'Course she's coming. Just think, Kerrie.' He stopped and waved his arm towards some place beyond the city and the ashen clouds. 'Tonight we could be away from here, right away. Tonight we could be up in the mountains.'

Part three
Finding Avalon

Three tickets north

Kerrie was getting anxious. Skip had been ages in the toilets and the train was due to leave in six minutes. Mauve had gone to buy tickets for their journey and there was no sign of her either.

'Where'll you say we're going to?' Kerrie had asked. 'We don't know yet. You canny just ask for three tickets up north somewhere.'

They had a quick look at a map of rail routes outside the ticket kiosk.

Skip had planted a finger on Inverness. 'That'll do. It's away up north and we can hunt out the monster for Mauve to paint.'

A group of boys in green blazers was emerging from the station toilets with Skip at their tail. The boys were shaking up cans of Coke and spraying each other with froth. Skip was watching their antics with a look on his face that Kerrie couldn't read. Two of the boys were about Skip's height but they surely couldn't be the same age, thought Kerrie, not with their wide-awake eyes and fine, baby complexions. Beside them, Skip's features were flint-sharp: a gash of mouth, dark eyes and hair, a pale, pointed face drawn with shadows, and that look as if he'd set his face against the wind. But that was just his public face. Kerrie now knew the smile that would crumple up his frown.

Skip was staring at something behind her. Kerrie turned and saw he was fixed on his own reflection in a photo-booth mirror. Once, he'd told her, when he hadn't seen his own reflection for months, he'd caught sight of a grumpy-faced wee tramp in a shop window and realized with a shock that it was himself.

Skip was up close at the photo-booth mirror now, baring his teeth in a toothpaste ad smile, scrabbling fingers in his hair. His hair was good, thought Kerrie, thick and skewy. 'All right,' he was mouthing at himself. He thought so too.

The mirror was greasy with fingerprints. Skip rubbed at it with the sleeve of his coat. Then he licked a finger and scrubbed at one cheek until tiny black rolls of dead skin rubbed away and there was a patch of raw pink.

'Oy, you're in a public place, remember.'

Skip started at Kerrie's loud hiss.

'And you've a dirty great tidemark round your chin. I've been meaning to tell you for a while to wash your neck.'

She was only kidding him on but he looked at her miserably.

'Do I look a mess?'

Kerrie felt a giggle rising. Mess was an understatement, but he was obviously upset by the green-blazer

116

boys. She slipped her hand into the back pocket of her jeans where she usually kept a comb, but instead of plastic teeth she felt the crackle of paper. Kerrie pulled out a creased envelope – her letter to Mum. She'd never posted it.

Kerrie turned her back to Skip to give herself a second to think. There was a bin right in front of her, and over by the newsagent's kiosk there was a postbox. She didn't have time to think. Mauve would be back any second. She'd just have to go on gut instinct and hope it was the right choice.

Skip was trying to read over her shoulder as she found a pen among her poly-bag full of bits and pieces and scribbled out Mum's name, care of Margaret's address.

'I'm leaving the city. Doing fine.' He read the words out loud as she scrawled them on the back of the envelope. 'So you are. Who's it to?' he asked. He knew fine well.

'My mum.'

'Thought she was dead or something.'

'That's my gran,' snapped Kerrie. Don't act stupid, she thought. 'You send a card to your mum and dad. You can buy them over there,' she said. Skip had never mentioned his parents and Mauve didn't seem to know much about his past. Or she wasn't telling. 'He doesny want to talk,' Mauve had said when Kerrie asked.

Mauve burst upon them now, her hands full of coins and crumpled tickets. 'Quick. Platform six. We've got about a minute left. The queue was a mile long.'

117

They bundled into a half-empty carriage and Skip immediately snuggled into a window seat. Kerrie couldn't sit, her legs felt as if they were itching.

She saw their shocked faces as she ran past their window. They thought she was scarpering off at the last minute. Kerrie raced to the postbox and shoved the letter in before she changed her mind. I should've sent a postcard to Shell, she thought, as the guard's whistle blew and she just made it in before the doors buzzed shut.

Skip leaned forward in his seat as a tremble of engine ran through the train and Kerrie settled herself, gasping for breath.

'This'll be brilliant,' he said. 'The best thing that's ever happened to me, and you nearly went and missed it.'

Kerrie giggled and fanned her hot face with her hat.

The train slid out of the dark cover of the station into an ashen grey drizzle. Here and there at the side of the track a tree flashed by in a blaze of autumn and its litter of leaves was caught up in their movement, in a great wheel of wind.

Kerrie wished that Skip's excitement could touch her. She was bothered by all sorts of unsettling thoughts. There was the letter she'd just posted. Kerrie tried not to dwell on the half-remembered things she'd spilled out in it that grey day at the park. Then there was the image of the woman in the street beside the alleyway this morning, that was bothering her too.

118

Kerrie scrubbed the thought of the woman from her mind. Something about the paper-seller, sitting in the cold beside a bundle of morning papers, something about her sad-clown cheeks and her raw, grazed skin, the skin of years of hard weather and city dirt, had made a chill in her stomach. And then Kerrie saw that it could be herself in years to come.

As the train relaxed into a steady rhythm Kerrie wondered if she would ever again feel safe and warm. Gran and the gang had been like a cosy blanket flung around her, insulating her from the outside world. Now Gran was gone and Kerrie had cast her friends aside. Her whole life had cracked right across and she'd stepped over the chasm into a new existence.

Kerrie felt a flush of shame as she remembered how cruel she had been to Shell last night. Shell must be badly worried, badly hurt too. She'd find a phone somewhere, talk to Shell and try to make it up to her. Somehow.

Skip was watching her. Kerrie turned so that he couldn't read her face, and saw the last scatterings of the city break up into fields. She didn't want to think about it all any more, about the muddle her life had become.

It was much simpler, for now, just to drift along with the rising line of the horizon, to relax and fall into the comforting rock of the train, and to tell herself she'd think about it all some time later when she wasn't so tired and achy, when her head was quiet and they were all settled some place up north, wherever that turned out to be.

'Wake up, you two. Quick, you're missing everything.'

Kerrie and Skip woke with a start. Skip stood up and looked around dazedly.

'Calm down. We're no' there yet. Just look though. Look at that,' said Mauve.

They gazed out the window. Nothing in their other lives had prepared them for the overwhelming nature of the scenery that they now travelled through.

'Where did that come from?'

'Where are we?'

To their right a massive, smooth-sweeping mountain rose to a conical peak clumped with small rain clouds.

'It's like a volcano. Maybe it's a dead volcano.'

'An upside-down ice-cream cone.'

'Poppy-seed bread.'

'Eh?'

'The loaves you get with the poppy seeds sprinkled on them,' explained Kerrie. 'Gran always got them for special teas. All the crumbly bits of rock down the sides look like poppy seeds.'

'You buy me a poppy-seed loaf and I'll see,' said Skip. 'Aw, yes!'

He crammed his face against the window as they crossed a high, wide-curving bridge which spanned a dizzying current of river, fed by the mountain burns. They were directly under the cone-shaped mountain now, the railway line cutting a path into its base. It was far wider and bigger, monstrously so, than it had appeared from just across the river.

'It feels like it's gonny topple. It's right over our heads.'

'Imagine there was a rock slide.'

Mauve was silently, frantically, sketching. Then, as an unexpected break appeared in the crowd of mountains, she sighed and stuck her pencil in her pocket, too mesmerized by the unfolding scene to do more than watch.

As abruptly as the mountains had closed in, the landscape now widened out, flat and desolate. Along the horizon sat a rim of dark mountains. And all before them sprawled a stretch of moorland, as vast as a sea, a wilderness blazing with autumn.

'I've never seen anything so empty,' whispered Kerrie. And so fierce, she thought, all that fire.

'Weird,' grunted Skip.

'There's so much.' Mauve sounded as if she had stopped breathing.

This must be heaven for her, thought Kerrie. She saw a shiver, a wave of something, pass through Mauve and knew she was deep in zombie mode. Then suddenly Mauve snapped out of her trance.

'Let's stop here,' she said.

. Kerrie looked at Skip, her mind a blank.

'There's so much out there.' Mauve stood up and rocked with the train.

Skip frowned, glanced again at the expanse of wind-blasted moor. Only black bog-puddles, the odd purple splash of heather and a few rocks the size of a bus interrupted the immense blaze of land. There was no sign of any living thing. 'So there is. There's a load of grass. A lot of air as well.'

'Please,' said Mauve.

Skip looked to Kerrie for help and she shrugged. How could they refuse? They were, after all, travelling on Mauve's money.

'What about the Highlands?' said Kerrie. 'That's where we paid to go to.'

'Well, this practically is.' Mauve began to gather up her things. 'We can always go further later. It's just – oh, I've got to. I've never seen anything like this place.'

There was a pull on the movement of the train, and in a few seconds they felt the train ease and slow up.

'I canny see a thing. What would you have a station out in the middle of nowhere for? It's like the end of the earth. Another planet,' said Skip.

Kerrie strapped her guitar over her back. 'Couldny be worse than last night, could it?'

'Last night there was people and dogs and *things*. There's nothing out there. No' a single thing.'

The panic on Skip's face was so sharp Kerrie expected him to turn stormy and refuse to get off. But his expression cleared a little as the station came into view.

It was tiny and immaculate, with a pink-pebbled platform and manicured flower-beds.

'Weird,' muttered Skip, but he began to follow them to the door.

Alone on the station platform, they watched the train disappear into a dip in the moor, then faced each other in a silence that was utterly empty but for the hollow, ghostly sound of the wind and the distant train.

'Don't know if I like this,' said Kerrie. The sound unnerved her as did that rim of bare, whaleback mountains.

Skip had a spaced-out look on his face.

'There'll be somebody around,' said Mauve, a waver on her breath.

The pebbles crunched. They jumped round. In the doorway of the station house was an elderly woman with hair so white and sculpted it looked like a blob of meringue. On her feet were fluffy carpet slippers that matched the pink platform pebbles.

'Can I help you? You look a bit lost,' she called.

Kerrie collected her wits.

'Is – is there anywhere to stay round here? A bed and breakfast or . . .' She tailed off, feeling ridiculous as she looked out over the wilderness.

The woman took a minute to look them over thoroughly.

'Come away into the tea room and we'll see. You look like you could murder some cheese toasties.'

Over a formidable pile of cheese toasties the woman chatted to them about her last visit to Glasgow, many years ago. She preferred Perth for shopping, she said, it wasn't such a trail, and not so busy as the city. The longer she chatted, though, it became clear that she was itching to know what three youngsters from the city were up to in such a desolate place.

Eventually, Mauve managed to satisfy her that they were all art students, on a sketching trip. The woman nodded, taking in Mauve's bin-bag full of paints and rolled-up canvases. They got a lot of students visiting, said the woman, but usually geology ones, to study the land. Or biology ones because of the plant life, she added, agreeing with Skip that there was certainly enough of both hereabouts.

'Of course, there's been a lot of changes round here lately,' the woman commented as the conversation dwindled.

They followed her gaze to the unbroken landscape through the window.

'This all used to be moorland,' she continued while they still looked out, searching for clues.

'It's the peat they're after now. They're having it all dug up and selling it in B & Q. And then there's the forestation. They've gone completely forest mad. Over that side it's all young trees now, but not a real forest. It's all pine and spruce. Grows in a year or two and ruins the land in the end, sucks out all the good in it, but it's easy money for the landowners. Year by year, one way and another, the moor's shrinking away under our noses.'

The woman got up to refill the teapot, and the three of them collapsed in giggles.

'Shrinking!' spluttered Skip. 'You canny see the end of it! And whose noses? There's nobody else out here.

She's probably half daft with the loneliness, poor woman.'

But the woman had returned with the tea and a leaflet.

'This'll help you. Though you've missed the bus to the village and there's not another one today.'

'Village?'

The woman looked puzzled at their surprise.

'At the other end of the loch. Now are you sure you're not lost? Did your college not get you sorted out with maps and accommodation? Anyhow, there's a list of bed and breakfasts here on the leaflet.'

She seemed uncertain now as if she sensed there was something amiss. She looked at Kerrie's guitar and their clutter of tatty plastic bags. Kerrie felt the woman take in her scruffy jacket and boots, Mauve's dripping jewellery and Skip's ridiculously large coat. It was a good three sizes too big for him, after all. Their attack on the cheese toasties must have made them look as if they were half-starved. And they all badly needed a sleep and a good scrub. The woman must suspect something odd – or perhaps they fitted her idea of eccentric art students.

'It's a good hour and a half's walk to the village so you should phone and book rooms. The phone's just over the bridge,' the woman instructed, still looking worried as she set them off in the right direction. 'I'd hurry or you'll be walking in the dark.'

Over the railway bridge on an empty hillside sat a red phone box.

Skip shook his head.

'Weird.'

'I think we should wait till we get there,' said Mauve.

'Get where?' he demanded.

'Wherever we get. It's just after five. We've plenty of time.'

'I need to phone,' Kerrie announced. 'It's Shell. I never got to tell her.'

'Think she'll want to speak to you?' asked Skip.

'Don't know,' Kerrie mumbled.

She took a moment before she dialled. Miserably, she felt the truth of what she'd blurted out so clumsily last night. For this was the first time in all the countless phone calls she'd made to Shell over the last couple of years that Kerrie wondered what on earth she would find to say.

The strangest of places

For a while after she'd cut herself off, Kerrie stayed shut in the phone box, the phone still held to her ear in case the others were looking. Tears stung her eyes and she struggled with them.

'How are you?' Shell had asked, polite and tight-voiced like she was some old auntie. Kerrie had tried to talk as normal, but the hurt she heard at the end of the line was raw.

'It's all too complicated, Shell. But I'm all right, honest,' she said.

There was hesitation, or a crackle, at the other end.

'That's good,' Shell replied, her voice flat and sheer as the moor rocks. 'So, are you coming back sometime? It's just so's we know whether to get a new guitarist or not.'

'Well, I don't know. Yes. It's all so strange.'

Silence, and the wind wailing over the desolate moor. A sigh?

Then Kerrie gathered up her courage. She poured out how sorry she was about the way she had spoken to

Shell last night, how much she missed everyone, how odd and frightened she felt in this new life with Skip and Mauve.

'But I'll be all right,' she promised. 'I'll keep in touch.'

'You'd better,' Shell said, sounding more like herself. 'Or I'll send mumping Margaret after you.'

And then there was a muffled struggle as Mrs McCormack seized the phone.

'Kerrie? Is that you, pet? I know it is. Now tell me where you are. Come on now, you've upset everyone enough. If you could see your mum, the state she's in, on the television and everything. If your gran was here . . . Kerrie? You come home and we'll sort all this out.'

The echo of the TV and a door slamming.

'Kerrie?'

When she rejoined Skip and Mauve, they were arguing over the map the woman had given them.

'That's the wrong way round, stupid. We follow this road till we come to the loch and the road follows the loch to the village. See?'

Skip grunted.

'But that means the village is away at the other end of the loch. I'm awful tired.'

'Tough,' snapped Mauve, whose face was drawn and heavy with lack of sleep. 'You got through then, Kerrie?'

They were both too preoccupied with the map to notice that she couldn't answer.

128

The rough track they were on soon evened out into a proper road, yet it was barely wide enough for a vehicle. As they took a sharp bend they realized that they had been on a hill, although the moor had appeared so flat, and the road dipped deep into a small valley.

'What's that?'

Skip had stopped dead, his eyes wide. He took a few tentative steps forward and stopped again, his expression intensifying.

A deep drumming came from the earth.

As they walked further round the bend, down into the valley, the drumming grew to a thunder until the ground and the rocks vibrated with it.

Skip glared accusingly at Mauve. He had the sparkly out, Kerrie saw. He held it tight in one hand, a little out in front of him, as if warding off any danger or evil spirits lurking in the thundering valley.

They crept further round the bend and saw what it was: a vast, dirty-cream curtain of water smashing into a pool of brown foam. The pool spewed the water out over rocks and boulders until it calmed much further on into a dark, steady current.

Skip slid the sparkly back into his pocket.

'There's a path.' Mauve began to clamber up the rocky slope that led to the top of the waterfall.

The path ended at a ledge where they could look down into the pool of savage foam. The noise was deafening and they had to clutch on to each other in the face of the blasting wind made by the crash of water.

'It's a dam,' Mauve shouted.

They looked over the top of the waterfall to the level surface of dammed water. Kerrie looked from one side to the other, at the two things that were of the same: the deathly-still dam and the roaring, mesmerizing violence.

'Nah. Daft idea. You're too young to die.'

His voice was so close to her ear it made her jump.

'What'd she say then?'

'Who?' Kerrie asked.

'Your pal.'

Kerrie shrugged. She wasn't going to yell at him over this racket.

Skip took her sleeve and pulled her back down the path until the thundering receded.

'You were right,' he said. 'She's still part of normal life. You're outside it now.'

'I know that,' Kerrie snapped.

Skip looked about him as if he could find faith or words from this alien new world.

'I just don't know if I can stick it,' said Kerrie. 'I mean, look at us, we don't even know where we're going tonight, never mind where we'll end up next month, next year.'

Skip broke into one of his rare, creased-up grins.

'Come on. Mauve'll make us famous in her paintings and I'll teach you to busk just in case she doesny. I promise you, this is gonny be good.'

There was a squelch and Skip was suddenly floundering about in a peat-bog, cursing the moor, the mountains, the rocks and anything else in his line of vision.

The sight of him black-spattered and glowering again broke Kerrie's mood and the laugh ached in her, an unused muscle.

Mauve was standing high on a rock.

'I can see the start of the loch. It's no' too far.'

'The *start* of the loch. Brilliant,' grumped Skip as he wiped himself with grass. 'We'll maybe get to the village in time for breakfast.'

The thought had them hurrying on to the road which followed the river until it suddenly spilled out into a wide mouth of water.

It was the strangest of places. Thousands of huge, ancient boulders littered the end of the moor as if a giant hand had hurled them across it in a fit of temper. In between the boulders grazed hundreds of sheep.

The loch was wide and waveless, and they could see no end to it. Deep green pines spread up the sides of the mountains and withered to scrunty trees by its shore. They were, along with the fiery blotches of fern and the scattering grey sky, all mirrored precisely on its still surface.

'Wow,' breathed Skip. 'It's big, eh? And awfy long,' he added, realizing he had to walk the length of it.

Kerrie heard the sound of a million pin-pricks hit the water and called at the other two to keep moving.

Beyond the mouth of the loch the road entered a long archway of trees whose delicate copper leaves draped to the ground like gold lace, sheltering them from the light rain. At the side of the road, almost hidden by a tendril of leaves, was a wooden signpost. It hung above a little circle of rocks.

'A wishing well,' whispered Kerrie. Something made her grab Skip's coat and pull him over with her to read the words on the signpost. She wasn't really surprised to find they were written in an unintelligible language.

Kerrie grew goosebumps. Everything had an other-wordly aspect to it. The unearthly nature of the moor, the vast mirror-stillness of the loch, and not a living soul anywhere. Now this. A mysterious signpost. And a strong roasted-earth smell suddenly in the air.

'Guest house.' Kerrie said it briskly to hide her relief. 'See, it's in English here.' The smaller lettering under-neath was hard to decipher in the gloom of the trees.

'So what's that other stuff say? How's it no' in English?'

Skip was doing his snail act.

Something moved at the back of Kerrie's mind, through her tiredness.

'Gaelic. I think it's maybe Gaelic. We're nearly in the Highlands, remember.'

Skip clapped her on the back.

'Course. I was getting the jitters there.' He laughed, and the sound was swallowed by the trees. 'I was think-ing we'd stepped into a fairy world and we'd – what is that?'

Beyond an ornate iron gate and up through a narrow alleyway of tall pines there was a slice of grey stone as tall as the trees that almost hid it from view. They opened the gate and crept up the path through the pines. At the end sat two stone lions guarding a steep run of crumbled stairs. Above the stairs they saw that the slice of stone had opened out into a large house whose pillared entrance, carved stonework and turret gave it the look of a small castle.

'They'll never take us,' said Skip, staring at the tiny window set in the turret's pointy hat as if he expected a witch to appear.

'Who'd live out here in the middle of nothing?' whispered Kerrie, her imagination casting up old horror films she and Gran had sat up watching late on Saturday nights. She began to examine the windows for ghoulish faces and then checked herself for being ridiculous. She always got creepy when she was over-tired.

'Nothing?' said Mauve. 'Kerrie, are you blind? There's everything out here.'

'They willny let us in,' insisted Skip. 'Look at us.'

They looked each other over, at their crumpled, peat-spattered clothes and grimy faces.

'You're the worst,' said Kerrie. 'You hide down the path.'

Skip raised an eyebrow. 'Think so?'

'Well, what'll we do? My legs willny move now they think there's maybe a bed here.'

'The loch,' said Mauve, and she ran off down the path through the pines.

'She would drive you demented,' said Kerrie. 'I'll fling that sketch pad of hers in the loch.'

'Nah, it's something else.' Skip ran off after Mauve. Kerrie groaned up at the patch of sky between the pines and the roof of the house and followed.

Mauve was scrubbing her hands and face with sand and water at the edge of the loch. She found a sharp-edged stone and scraped some of the mud from her jeans, then kicked her boots about in the water. She turned round and bowed.

'Freezing,' she squeaked.

She sat on a rock wiggling water from her feet while the other two splashed about.

They squelched up to the guest house arguing over who should do the talking. But as they reached the front steps there was movement behind the glass door, then a girl opened it. She looked extremely ordinary.

'Yes?'

'We wondered if you had any rooms. For the night,' said Mauve.

The girl took in their sodden clothing.

'I will ask. For one night?'

'Oh.'

Mauve looked at Kerrie.

'Aye. Yes. Thanks.'

The girl disappeared somewhere down the long hallway.

'She must be Gaelic,' said Skip. 'Funny accent.'

A very large man walked towards them.

'Good evening.' He smiled. His voice was soft for

someone so big. It hushed into the plush carpets and wallpaper. 'But sorry, we do not take hillwalkers. You can go to the village, please. Excuse me.'

He shut the door on them. Skip rang the doorbell. The man looked through the glass.

'We're no' hillwalkers,' called Skip. 'Mauve's an artist and we're musicians. We've loadsa money on us. We can pay you up front. Mauve's just sold a bunch of paintings and she's up here to paint the mountains and stuff 'cause . . .'

Kerrie cut in before he yelled their whole life story at the man. 'We only want to stay the night. Please. We're really tired, we've come all the way from Glasgow. We'll take our boots off and not muck up your carpets and stuff.'

The man opened the door. He hesitated a moment, looked them over thoroughly, then smiled.

'Excuse me,' he said, and disappeared down the hall. They could hear voices then a moment later he returned. 'I think we have enough room for an artist and musicians,' he said. 'My friends are here to visit Scotland and would like to meet such interesting Scottish people. But please take all shoes off and carry them upstairs. Along here I have two nice rooms.'

They were led up a staircase. Skip poked Kerrie in the back.

'Two rooms? Why two? Does that mean,' the wonderful idea hit him, 'that he's giving me a room to myself? Does it?'

'Probably,' said Kerrie, who found the thought of

sharing with Mauve more of a thrill after years, and especially after these last weeks, of sleeping alone.

Skip quietly yelped.

Gingerly, Skip prodded the lemon quilt on his bed then smoothed the minute dent he'd made on it. A whole double bed. He shook his head. Incredible. 'And there's more,' he told Kerrie, as if she couldn't see for herself.

'I've already said, our room's got all that as well. Mauve's just run a bubble bath you could suffocate in, it's so high,' said Kerrie.

'Aye, but youse've got to share your biscuits and stuff,' he said. 'I've got everything all to myself.'

Skip carried on showing off his room, fingering each item as he listed it off to her, as if he were memorizing every detail as he went along. There was a desk in front of the window with a notepad and pen, a Teasmade on the dressing table with a tray of milk, sugar and biscuits, and a polished, full-length mirror on the front of the wardrobe. In the tiny adjoining bathroom there was soap, soft toilet paper, clean, white towels and sachets of bubble bath and shampoo.

Skip touched each thing gently as if it might crumble or vanish. Then he sat down on the bed, forgetting about the creases. He looked close to tears.

'Calm down,' said Kerrie. She patted his hand, not knowing what else to do.

In a way it was the cruellest thing that could have happened to him, she thought. How was he to go back to shop doorways or building sites now? He'd always want this, a wee world of his own.

Skip went into the bathroom and wiped his eyes on a piece of toilet paper, then went over to the window. Half of it was covered by the slope of the turret next to his room. But beyond that there was a view that was just as magical as the view from the rooftop. There was a long slope of lawn, then the mass of pines that hid the guest house from the road. Over the dark tips of the trees was the loch, the cragged line of mountains and the sky, all flame and ash now, the grey of the day warmed to embers by the sunset behind the clouds.

Skip turned back to survey his room once again. He switched on the bedside lamp.

'Bath, bed, Teasmade, desk,' he chanted. 'Right then, I'll run a bubble bath and sit in it with some tea and a chocolate biscuit,' he decided, looking pleased at his ingenuity in combining several luxuries in one go.

Kerrie left him to it and went to explore what she could of the house and its grounds until Mauve gave her a turn of their bathroom.

A world before cities

From a nearby room there came laughter and loud voices.

'I heard them all talking Gaelic when I was coming down the stairs,' Skip whispered. 'There's a lot of them.'

The tall man entered the room, introduced himself as Otto and said he hoped they would like German food.

'You are here in the small dining room because we are all German and we talk very loud, all together,' he explained. 'It's nicer for you in here, yes?'

He smiled and nodded. They nodded back.

'German food?' said Skip.

'Yes,' said Otto. 'But we can make omelette or . . .'

'Nah,' said Skip. 'We'll have the German stuff, thanks.'

'German,' repeated Kerrie, as Otto left. 'Here?'

'You were close, mind,' said Skip. 'Begins with a "G".'

'Weird,' said Mauve.

'Everything,' pronounced Skip, 'is weird out here. I'm getting used to it.'

The soup arrived. In the middle of each bowl sat a large island of puff pastry.

'See?'

He picked up the pastry in his fingers and sooked the soup out of it.

'He's an embarrassment,' muttered Kerrie. 'Stop that.'

Skip ignored her, drinking his soup in great gulps.

'I think I'd like Germany.' Kerrie gave a great yawn. She'd just finished the last bite of a large slice of apple and honey cake and all she could think about now was sinking into that pile of pillows on her soft, squeaking bed. 'Just think, we'd've been in a hostel tonight. Or stood on a pavement having a roll and chips.' She yawned again. 'I give in. Night-night.'

'We'll go exploring in the morning,' she heard Skip say as she dragged her feet up the stairs. 'The loch and everything.'

Was the whole world like this before cities? Kerrie wondered, as Mauve sketched the lochside scenery. You could watch Mauve work for hours, she thought, watch her pick out some warped or magical aspect from the most ordinary things.

There was a rock at the edge of the water that on Mauve's sketch pad became squat and bulldog-like. The mountain opposite, its rocks protruding through russet and green, took on the look of a skeletal old woman gowned in velvet, and a dead tree near the mouth of the loch with a branch poised like a foot appeared stilled as if by some ancient spell as it ventured out on to the moor.

The German party had left early for a day's touring and Otto had sat down with the three of them at breakfast for a chat. Kerrie's curiosity had finally overcome her shyness, and Otto had explained, in answer to her questions, that his wife had been Scottish and it had been her idea to open up their guest house some years ago, to sell holidays in a Scottish wilderness to German tourists. It had proved a resounding success but, sadly, his wife had died last year. His daughter helped out during her holidays from college.

'Shame,' said Kerrie, as they'd headed down to the lochside, energized by a breakfast of muesli, eggs, bacon, and a platter of German meats and cheeses. 'He's an awful nice guy.'

Skip had decided that it was high time he began to train Kerrie up in her new career as a busker. But at the moment he lay stretched out on the damp sand of the tiny lochside beach watching the sun burn rolls of cloud off the surface of the loch. He was muttering to himself.

'I'm as high as the clouds. How'd we get so high? If you went up that mountain on a day like this it would be the best thing in the world. The best.'

Kerrie nudged him with her foot, ready with her guitar. 'Come on back to earth. I'm fed up waiting.'

She had to wait some more while Skip dragged his thoughts to ground level. He yawned, sat up, and fixed his eyes on a blue patch between two clouds as he blew a few warm-up blasts into his mouth organ. Then Kerrie was left to fend for herself with her guitar as he started to work through his repertoire of folk songs.

It was like trying to jump into a game of skipping ropes, she thought. Every time she tried to join in, she would find herself in a tangle of chords and would have to unravel herself and hover at the edges until she managed to find a way into the pattern again. Gradually, she found her own space in the music. After a time, they both heard something and stopped.

Mauve was engrossed, torn from her work.

'Go on. Don't stop or you'll lose it.'

As the sun gleaned the last of the frost haze and a deep blue settled on the loch, they began to track the flickering thing in the music.

'If you stop thinking about it, that's when it works. As soon as I think, I lose it,' said Kerrie. She lay back on the sand, watching a puff of baby cloud. They began again. But this time as her eyes followed the cloud, she let her fingers steal at Skip's unworldly melodies from the rooftop, blending them with the folk melodies he played on his mouth organ.

Skip stopped, and there was only the lap of water on rock. He shifted.

'I was supposed to be teaching you these,' he said. 'But that's so weird it's brilliant.'

There was a colour to it, Kerrie was thinking. If she

could just find it and fall into it then the music would sort itself out, she was sure.

That evening, after another momentous meal and an entertaining chat with the German guests, Skip pestered until Kerrie agreed to go out for a walk. He wanted to find the village at the far end of the loch. Mauve decided she'd better come too as they'd have to begin to search for a cheaper place to stay. The guest house bill was going to make a sizeable dent in her wad of money.

But they had walked less than ten minutes from the guest house when Skip became intrigued by a path. It led deep into the heart of the dark pine forest that lurked behind the delicate auburn drape of the birch trees that lined the road. Skip began his pestering act again until the other two gave in and followed him.

Within a few steps they were swallowed into ancient forest. It crammed to either side of the path, held back as if by a crowd barrier. Generations of pine needles crumbled to dust on the forest floor. Not a bird chirped, no light or movement was within that gloom. Only their movements and the fizz of midgie clouds interrupted a silence that was emptier and louder than the one they'd heard at the station on the edge of the moor.

Kerrie imagined them to be a band of travellers from centuries past, trekking ancient pathways to some mysterious destination in the dim, greenish light that held the grass and the trees and was hazed by insects. Autumn would never reach this place.

The day's music had left her feeling as if she were crackling inside. She glanced at Skip. He looked like he'd had a dose of the sparkly. She watched him pick up a pine cone at his feet and break it open. He drew back at the whiff of concentrated forest, of ever-green springtime, that escaped from it.

As the path climbed, it twisted, and shadows grew at their feet. Looking back, Kerrie blinked in a chip of hard, gold sun. Wings fluttered overhead. She stood dazzled by the light, sensing something extraordinary like a bursting happiness. The forest had relaxed its guard for a moment to let in a chink of the outer world and the effect was of a mighty clash of forces. If she could only take away the essence of this strange moment, gather all the rays of the sunset and the mysterious power of the forest and press them into something small that she could pocket and keep with her for the bad times.

The state she's in.

Mrs McCormack's voice came at her again, this time from somewhere deep in the forest. Kerrie had been trying to shut her up these last few days but she kept echoing at her from all sorts of places – from the rocks around the loch, from deep inside the pine trees around the guest house or under the bed. It didn't matter how careful Kerrie was, Shell's mum would wait around for an unguarded moment then start off.

Anyhow, what Mrs McCormack had said couldn't be

true. Kerrie knew she was just a bit of stray luggage for Mum, she had been for years; and there was Phil now. Kerrie shoved away the uncomfortable image that Mrs McCormack had just presented to her of Mum opening up and reading the letter Kerrie had posted at the railway station. Well, she would just not think about it, Kerrie decided. She just wouldn't. There was no point.

Skip and Mauve waited for her round the curve of the path. They looked fuzzy in the grainy light.

'Come on,' said Skip. 'I want to get a view before it's dark.'

Without warning the forest had stopped and the sky gaped above them, chipped now with frozen stars. Kerrie searched patches of the sky but there was too much of it. Grandpa's star had been easy to locate when there had only been a strip of sky. And she'd never find Gran in all that.

They climbed on until the air was like mint in their throats and they were at a place where the valley swung out below them, almost as wide as the sky. The sun slipped under the loch as the moon rolled round the cone mountain and eyed its reflection in the water. Peat smoke from the village at the far end of the loch and from scattered cottages gathered and curled above the valley like the fumes of a sleeping dragon. A dragon guarding against the thing that lay at the edge of it all, waiting with the suck of a tide, thought Kerrie, then wondered why on earth this had come to her.

Skip broke the silence.

'Doo'd be in heaven here. I wish he'd come.' He drew

a deep breath and let it out in a great creamy cloud. 'Mauve, we've got to get us a place here, then maybe I can go and bring Doo up. You can paint me for hours in the freezing cold, as long as you like, and I'll sit as still as a stone, I will.'

Mauve stood looking at the moon in the loch.

'There's a place,' she said slowly. She started back off down the hillside, tripping over a loose rock as she went. 'I think there is. Come on and see.'

The moor plays

Mauve had spotted a truck tyre on the grass verge at the roadside with CARAVAN TO LET white-painted round its rim. They asked at the nearby farmhouse and were directed to a small spur of hill that overlooked the road to the village. The woman at the farm told them they'd find the caravan up there if they wanted to look it over. She was incredulous that anyone, even a group of tatty art students from Glasgow, would want to spend the winter with only the thin walls of a caravan between them and the wilderness outside, and agreed to an extremely low rent. The caravan was theirs till the early spring.

Skip locked himself in his bedroom after tea on their last evening at the guest house. He said he wanted peace to have a long bath, and Kerrie heard the sound of him topping it up over and over again with hot water as she lay on her bed with her toes warming at the radiator. She closed her eyes and smelled the old wood of the wardrobe, the comfortable mustiness of the room, mixed with the peat-reek and faint cooking smells from downstairs.

Skip had said he wanted something, a memento, of this special place. What did he mean? A face flannel or an ashtray? Kerrie had watched him pull open all the dressing-table drawers. He knew they were empty. He'd already explored every corner of his room. Then he'd rechecked the wardrobe. But there had been nothing except a few coat hangers.

Kerrie jumped as someone hammered on her door. She opened it and there was Skip wrapped in a large peach bath-towel.

'Look!'

She looked at the book he waved in her face as he pushed past her and sat himself down.

He'd been lying on his bed after his bath. There was a breeze from the window he'd opened a crack to let in the scent of the pines outside. It lifted the ends of the heavy curtain – the window ledge had been the one place he hadn't thought to look – and he'd glimpsed something dark behind it. A book.

Skip handed Kerrie the book as if it were made of crystal. Its green-bound cover was thready with age, its pages tindery. She opened it and the movement interrupted the dust caught in its ancient pages. She sneezed. 1938. *Moorland Tales*.

'Brilliant, eh?' Skip smiled.

The caravan was too small for the three of them, but it had a cosy feel to it. A two-ring gas cooker sat beside the sink, in between the bedroom areas, and doubled up as a heater that nicely warmed up their cramped space. The whole caravan was kitted out in aged olive green and pink throughout, from its frilled curtains and the bedclothes for their foldaway beds to the dusty pink roses on the glass paraffin lamps. Yuk, Mauve shuddered, but she was really quite pleased with herself for finding them such a comfortable home for the winter.

Outside their door was the ever-present soundtrack of several hundred sheep. There was food on their doorstep too: eggs, sheep's cheese, bread, potatoes and milk from the farmhouse and, occasionally, fish from Otto's Sunday afternoon boat trips out on the loch. They had freezing, peaty water from any number of burns, and bonfires at dark. And there was the wide stretch of the loch valley to gaze at.

As soon as they moved in, Mauve started to disappear in the mornings before the other two were up. She would return as darkness fell and join them round the bonfire for lumps of toasted cheese, cold to the bone, tired and apologetic, promising she'd spend more time with them once the ideas settled down. But they could see she was lodged in some other dimension and that she was intensely, feverishly happy.

Kerrie groaned. It was only eight o'clock in the morning and Skip was banging about at the cooker at the end of her bed. At least Mauve was quiet when she got up. Kerrie preferred to stay in the cosy huddle of her bedclothes during the mornings as she was finding there was nothing much to do once she got up.

The rising shriek of the boiled kettle cut through the last of her sleep and Kerrie sat up. She could hear the sheep, who nosed around the caravan all day, run off down the hill as if they thought it was the starter whistle in a cross-country race. You'd think after three weeks they'd get wise, thought Kerrie. Skip had launched into his role of race commentator, watching the sheep from the window above the sink.

'And they're off. Jemima's in the lead but Sporran's at her tall and – whoa, there's been a disaster. The lot of them've skidded into a bog-puddle, never remember to swerve it, the pea-brains.'

Kerrie giggled and pulled on her clothes.

'What exciting things will we do today then?' she asked.

Skip handed her a mug of tea and some toast, and gave her an irritated look.

After breakfast, Kerrie stretched out on her bed again and listened to the sheep nosey around the caravan and complain to each other. She was utterly bored and yet she couldn't think of a reason to go out. Skip was reading out bits of his precious book that he found interesting.

'I've heard it a hundred times,' snapped Kerrie.

'A hundred? You been counting?' said Skip. 'Funny, that's the first time I found that bit. What's up with you?' He turned back to his book. He didn't really want an answer, he just wanted her to give him peace, Kerrie knew. She couldn't, though.

'Here we are then.'

She picked up the mouth organ he'd left lying on the fold-out table in the caravan's tiny kitchen area and made an attempt to imitate the sheep on it. That would surely annoy him.

'We're stuck, you know. In the middle of nowhere.' Kerrie managed a bleat that sent the sheep scattering.

Skip sighed. 'In the middle of everywhere.'

'I mean it,' said Kerrie.

'Aye.'

She flung a cushion at him.

'Skip.'

'What?' he yelled. He looked at her. 'Listen, you. I love it here.' He snatched the mouth organ out of her fingers and stuffed it in his pocket.

'So do I, but . . .'

'But?' he demanded. 'Your trouble is you've been spoilt. If you'd been on the streets for years like me and Mauve you wouldny be bored, you'd be loving this too. So shut up and give me peace to enjoy myself.'

Your trouble, thought Kerrie, is you're so used to drifting you'll settle for any kind of life as long as you've a place to stay. She took off her watch and laid it on the table. 'Shell invented this 'cause she was always bored and itching for some action. You get exactly five minutes and you think up something interesting to do. You have to clear your head first.'

It was a long, restless five minutes, and she knew Skip was only humouring her.

'Well?'

'Nothing,' yawned Skip.

'Nothing at all?'

'You?'

'I don't know.' Kerrie flung his coat at him. 'I need a walk. Come on.'

They struggled through gawping sheep and made for the hatchet-shaped rock that was wedged in the shoulder of the hill up beyond the caravan.

'It's limbo,' said Kerrie at last.

'What is?' asked Skip.

'This.'

She opened her arms to the loch valley.

'I thought it was more like heaven,' he said.

'There's no such thing as heaven on earth. My gran said. That's why we're stuck. In limbo you can't move.' Kerrie leaned against the hatchet rock and dug her heel into the soft ground at the side of a peat-bog. 'So, are we planning on hanging out with a bunch of sheep all winter? We'll end up as daft as they are by the end of it – at least, I will.' She made a perfect footprint in the black peat-bog.

Skip began to walk back down the hill.

He turned back.

'I'm sick of fighting against things. I used to like it 'cause when it hurt I knew I was alive. Most of the time I didny feel anything. Here, I'm making songs, eating proper food, seeing a bit of the world, and you think it's nothing. Feels like living to me.' He was off again.

Kerrie kicked the peat, spoiling her footprint.

'Listen,' she called after him.

'No.'

She ran to catch up with him as he tried to cross a burn.

'Just give me a minute. I've a plan. I worked it all out from your book.' There was a flicker of interest from him at this.

'I just need to do something or I'm scared I'll cave in and go back. I keep thinking about my mum. Shell's mum said . . .' Kerrie sighed. 'Things.'

Skip stared at his muddy feet. 'I wanted to send for Doo. I could make him come up, I could.'

'There's hardly room for the three of us in that caravan,' protested Kerrie. 'And he's old. He should be warm in a house over the winter, like he said. We could just move on for a while, just till I feel sorted out. We've got the songs, we could do something now, busking, I know we could,' Kerrie argued against his flat silence. 'But this sitting around – all I do is think. I need to move, do something. The thought of all winter . . .'

An unnerving memory of Gran interrupted Kerrie's argument. Gran, sitting on her bed, a long time ago. 'She's not bad, Kerrie,' she was saying. 'Your mum's just run away from her problems instead of looking them in the face. She's in a trap, she has to keep moving or it'll all catch up with her.'

'What about Mauve?' Skip was asking.

Kerrie shivered and cleared her throat. 'Mauve's all right, she's no' bothered about anything but her painting. That stuff about our faces – she knows our faces off by heart. And we canny keep living off her. We've got to shift ourselves and find our own way, find what we can do. Like she has.'

Skip gave a weighty sigh.

'We'd come back soon, promise,' said Kerrie. 'We'd never lose touch with Mauve.'

'What's this plan then?' Skip asked.

He took his book out of a coat pocket, and smoothed his fingers over the ancient cover, as he always did, as if ironing out an imagined wrinkle. He handed it to Kerrie and she found the page with the map. She showed him a track, clearly marked, that led across the moor to the main road artery north. They could hitch the short distance to the nearest town and go for a busk.

'The train'd be easier,' said Skip.

'But it's all mountains up that way, for ages; this way, over to the west, there's towns we can busk in. See.' She showed him on the map.'

Skip fidgeted.

'Uh-uh,' he said. 'But what about that thing – the moor. We'd have to walk over it. It's a monster of a thing.'

Kerrie knew it was. She had tried to avoid the thought of that rim of silent, whaleback mountains and the empty expanse of the moor. It could suck someone into it and never spit them out again, just as the sea had with Dad. You'd count for no more than a blade of grass in all that. And to walk right into it would be the bravest thing she could do. Anyway, she had made her plan, and she wouldn't think about it. She would not let her fear stop her. She had forgotten Skip was just as terrified of the moor, though.

'Maybe, if we went into the emptiest place in the world we could manage anywhere after that,' she said. 'At least we could try.'

Water gulped over rocks as they stood staring at a peat-bog.

Skip groaned and kneeled to examine the map of bright yellow lichen covering a small rock at his feet.

'I'll think about it,' he said. 'And that's all I'm saying.'

The sky was still patched with dark night clouds as they left the caravan. Mauve had come back so late last night they'd given up on her and gone to bed. She was so deep in sleep she couldn't be roused so they left her a long, scribbled letter stuck to the door of the food cupboard.

By the time they reached the end of the loch the sun was burning swathes of early morning mist off the water and the sky was a brand-new, never-ending blue.

Kerrie felt a bursting joy. She put her face to the sun, opened her arms wide and let wild happiness stream through her. Then she had to run. She grinned at Skip, who was shaking his head at her, laughing.

'Race you,' she yelled. 'Last one on the moor gets dumped in a peat-bog.'

Pulling and shoving each other, they ran laughing on to the moor that lay wide open before them like the gateway to a new world.

Now, only a few hours later, it was beginning to seem that this was the only world there had ever been. There was no end to it, nothing else on earth. Kerrie wondered if they were walking in circles. The moor was playing with them. It had looked so straightforward on the map. The path must have disintegrated somewhat in the half century or so since Skip's book had been published.

'Have we been here before?'

Skip couldn't hear her for the wind.

Kerrie tried to believe that there were cities, multitudes of people, existing just a dozen miles from this eternity of wilderness. She tried to remember the rooftop, life in the flats, Gran, Shell, the band.

Thready rain intensified against her forehead and it was all she could do to believe in Skip, a few steps in front. Each time Kerrie looked up her heart jumped: it was so big, so endlessly big. It was still a fine day at the loch, she'd bet. As soon as the moor had lulled them into a false sense of security with calm sweeps of land and sky it had started to act up, first with the path and now with the weather. Stupid, she told herself, we should've checked, should've phoned for a weather forecast. The red phone box on the hill by the train station loomed in her mind's eye like a lifebuoy in a stormy sea.

Skip had fixed his gaze a step beyond his feet, watching for the traps of dead tree roots that wormed out of the peat. At the top of the bend they stopped. Another cairn, or was this the same one again? They peered at the metal inscription on the base of the cone of rocks.

THOMAS McCARRON
SHEPHERD
1886

The last one had been inscribed to unnamed soldiers, killed in battle on the moor, no date. A busy place this once; a lot busier than it was now.

Kerrie's boots were muddy and sodden, the path long having disintegrated into peat-marsh. She looked up.

'We're in a cloud.'

Skip was looking in bewilderment at a stunted tree that grew out of a crack in a solid rockface.

The peaty grass dribbled with moisture, it tried to suck her feet down with every step. All around, a hundred streams gushed like raw wounds and gathered in a roar further down the hillside. And they were being drenched by the gentle, ice-cold rain of the cloud.

'I think we're near a river. If we followed it . . .' Kerrie suggested. 'I've never been so wet in all my existence. I've never seen so much wet.' She attempted a laugh.

Skip turned and looked at her like he'd never seen

her before and was swallowed by a denser patch of cloud. Kerrie lunged for him and grabbed a piece of coat.

'We'd better eat something.'

She pulled him down beside the cairn and unstrapped her guitar from her back. She had packed food into the spaces inside its leather cover. Kerrie unzipped the cover, found cheese and bread, and handed a chunk of each to Skip.

This morning she had thought herself so clever and organized. Fine weather, food packs, the path across the moor marked in red pencil in Skip's precious book. Now Kerrie wondered how she could have been so stupid. No waterproofs, no compass, no means of shelter. And nobody but Mauve, lost in her own world somewhere around the loch, knew they were out here. In their letter they'd promised to telephone the farm-house to let her know where they'd got to, but it could be days before she'd start to worry. Kerrie watched Skip eating as if he was in a dream.

'I don't know where you are but you're scaring me. All this is scaring me stupid. It's beating us and you're helping it.'

'Scared?' asked Skip. His voice was as cold as rock.

'Terrified.' Kerrie shuddered. 'It was a crazy idea. You should never've listened to me.'

Skip stood up. 'I need a drink.'

'Take your pick,' said Kerrie, giggling through shudders, as Skip listened to the hillside and located the nearest burn.

157

Skip crouched on a rock and drank gulps and gulps of cold, brown water. He splashed his face and looked up at her. The cloud that had enveloped them was starting to clear.

'I'm all better now,' he said.

'Skip. Over there.'

He looked, following Kerrie's stare.

The cloud was dissolving fast and as the hillside cleared they saw something. Skip was breathing hard, making a white fog over Kerrie's shoulder.

In front of them a boat hung in midair.

Then, soft-focused in trails of white mist, there emerged a tree and a shore. They giggled at each other in relief.

'If there's a loch with a boat, there must be people somewhere,' said Skip.

They watched the cloud retreat over an empty loch valley. The boat sat lifeless on grey water as if fixed in cement. Skip kneeled in the wet grass and put his head in his hands.

'Some divine Avalon,' he groaned.

'What's that?'

'In my book. It was the place . . .'

'No, that,' said Kerrie.

A child's sobbing became the burble of water over rocks.

'I'm getting the shakes.' Skip stood up.

'I think we should go back and try and find the rail . . .' The scream was behind them.

'What is it?'

'I don't know.'

Wind played on the grass and the boat sat motionless.

'Keep moving,' said Kerrie.

Another scream, nearer, mixed with their own this time. They clutched on to each other as a large bird rose from the grass with its heart-rending screech.

'Keep moving.'

Further on they descended into a flat, wide hollow in the land, so marshy that Kerrie wondered if it had once held a loch. There was a crowd of giant boulders in the centre and the air moved with the fizzle of midgies. Skip took his book from his coat pocket and beat his way through. He'd seen them hang over the bins at the flats like this, he said, but it was too cold for midgies in this freezing mist. What were they wanting here?

A small sound that had been annoying Kerrie suddenly intensified. She peered up through the midgie clouds to the ridge of hill they'd just descended from and saw something move against the sky. She stepped backwards and slipped on slimy grass as the crack of gunshot echoed round and round the hollow in the moor.

'Deer. It maybe would be, eh?' Skip suggested.

'There's somebody out there, somewhere. Maybe we should try shouting,' said Kerrie. They tried, but the moisture in the drenched air seemed to absorb the sound, as if they were shouting inside a cardboard box.

Two great legs of sunbeam appeared, moving over the mountain behind them like searchlights. They blinked as the colours of the moor switched to a more intense fire and the soaking grass winked thousands of crystal lights. Just as suddenly the lights switched off and they fell back into wilderness. There was something cruel now in that line of hill, in that angle of light.

'Get out of here. Quick, come on.' Skip was running, floundering for direction. He was running anywhere. He found a slope and scrambled up. Kerrie followed at a calmer pace.

'What's up with you?' she asked.

He stood with sweat on his face, watching the hollow.

'What was all that about?' Kerrie scanned the moor for whatever it was that had frightened him.

'Something terrible.' Skip gulped in breaths.

'What?'

'A terrible thing,' he wheezed. He took the sparkly out of his pocket to ward off whatever it was.

'Where?' asked Kerrie.

'Down there.'

Kerrie looked. 'There's nothing.'

Skip wiped his lip. 'I'm telling you. It's horrible. I felt it.'

Kerrie sighed and found a rock to sit on.

'We're exhausted and we're hungry. You've got the jitters, there's nothing. I'm looking, and there's nothing there.'

'I felt it,' he insisted.

'I tell you what, think about a chicken curry. I

guarantee it'll take your mind off it,' said Kerrie, with a groan as she rubbed her empty stomach.

Skip continued to watch the hollow. He picked up a small rock and aimed it at a peat-bog.

'All right,' he muttered. 'Chicken curry and a cheese-burger. Remind me, whose daft idea was this?'

'Oh . . .'

'I forget the reasoning. Remind me. And a pie and burning hot Bovril from the van. I can just about taste it.'

Kerrie stood up.

'First thing, as soon as we get somewhere civilized, that's what I'm having. If we survive this; except we won't. We never thought of that, eh, Kerrie? My jaw hurts. It needs exercise. It hasny chewed anything for hours.'

'Shoosh. I saw something.'

Skip followed Kerrie's stricken stare towards the boulders in the valley below them.

'I think I did,' said Kerrie.

'A hillwalker,' he suggested.

'No.'

'No. Ah, let's get out of here.'

Kerrie shivered, then laughed. 'I'm probably starting to hallucinate.'

'Maybe. Shoo!' Skip shouted. He took out his mouth organ and began to rasp wildly on it as he backed along the ridge.

'Well, if I was a ghost that'd sure sort me out,' said Kerrie. 'I don't think.'

'Ghost? You said hallucinating.'

Kerrie stared hard at the spot.

'What would a ghost be doing out here?' said Skip. 'There's nobody to haunt.' He whipped his arms about as if ghosts could be swatted away like midgie clouds.

'If it's where the terrible thing happened,' said Kerrie.

'What terrible thing?'

'Your terrible thing. You said.'

'I didny see anything, though. It's this freaky moor.' Skip began to flip. 'I want off it. I want a nice, ordinary doorway for the night and a bag of chips.'

One of the roving sunbeams found them and they were caught in its bursting light. Again the moor sparkled like a sea of fiery crystals. The sunbeam faded and it was as if a heavy curtain had been drawn across the sky.

Kerrie felt her skin prickle as she peered into murkiness, her eyes still dazzled by the light. There was a blurred feeling to the world now, as if things had shifted ever so slightly out of focus. The slope of the moor, the great boulders in the hollow, the thick sky – it was all exactly the same. And yet not.

Heart hammering, Kerrie watched the moor. They had disturbed something, she and Skip, something that had lain here a long time. It was gathering up now, rising like a midgie cloud from the sodden grasses of the moor. In front of them, a denseness began to take form, became a standing shadow. The shadow solidified.

162

Kerrie found herself staring into the fierce, frightened face of a girl her own age.

The girl looked part of the moor, like the deer. She was stained the colour of the peaty burns and her clothes were mottled grey like the rocks. Wild, peat-brown hair hung in a tangle past her elbows.

Hair like Shell's, thought Kerrie. Don't run.

The girl backed away, watching them closely. She had the small, animal movements of a bird or a mouse. Her feet were wrapped in sodden material that tied round each ankle. One foot was stained the burnt red of old blood.

Slowly, Kerrie eased herself to the ground and motioned to Skip to do the same. The fear in the girl's eyes mirrored her own.

'Don't you dare shoo her.' Kerrie barely moved her lips. But he was fidgeting; no, something behind him was slithering through the grass.

The girl called out something. Her voice had a rough scrape in it. In an instant the rocks and the grass sprouted figures. They stood armed with scraps of dead tree. The girl called again and as the figures crept upon them Kerrie saw they were only small children.

'I think we should do some quick talking. They've got us trapped like a couple of rabbits,' breathed Skip.

'We're friends,' tried Kerrie. 'We've lost the path.' She gestured to the vast moor.

'Campbells,' hissed one of them and their advance quickened.

The girl by the boulder called out and the other children stilled. Her eyes met Kerrie's, angry now.

'Tell your king we're uncrushed yet. He wants more than twa keelies creeping about in the bogs to hae our heads.'

'Heads? What king? What's she . . . ?' began Skip.

'Shh!' Kerrie was trying to keep eye-contact with the girl.

'They're tinkers. Look at them, they're filthy, don't even know what year they're in. Don't even know it's a queen we've got,' muttered Skip.

'Will you shut up?' Kerrie whispered.

The children crept closer, straining to hear the intense conversation between the two crouched in the grass.

'I know what year I'm in,' said Skip.

Kerrie stood up.

'It's all right.' She tried to smile at the girl.

A small child touched her arm. Kerrie smiled down, then felt her knees buckle. She was on her back, pinned flat, while hands stripped her of her watch, hat and jewellery.

There was a scampering into silence.

Kerrie saw an empty sky. She sat up and looked around. The blurriness was clearing from the world around. She felt her guitar, strapped tight and safe, digging into her back. Beside her in the grass Skip fingered his forehead.

'A wee thing, a tiny wee thing walloped me with his stick,' he gasped. The look of outrage on his face switched to fear as he rummaged in his pockets and in the grass around him.

Skip struggled to his feet and stared at the empty moor.

Kerrie buried her face in her knees.

'They got my sparkly,' she heard him say at last. 'And my book. And my moothie. Everything.'

There was silence and finally Kerrie looked up. Skip sat still as a rock with tears streaming down his face. Minutes passed and he didn't move or make a sound, just sat, crying soundlessly, staring out at the moor.

Kerrie cleared the lump from her throat.

'It's all my fault. I made you come. I'll get your things back. I promise I will.'

She had no idea how she was going to set about finding a bunch of ghost children in all this moor. Frightened and dangerous ghosts too.

Kerrie hauled Skip to his feet and tried to ignore the prickle of fear that ran down her back as she faced the blank wilderness of the moor.

Fire and laser

A fevered sun had broken through in the last hour of daylight, turning the autumn grasses of the moor into a sea of fire. With the landscape suddenly clear and open, Kerrie was able to map out an imaginary path from the sunset pouring over the mountains to the west, right along to the smoother land directly opposite. The loch was to the east of the moor, she knew that, and they had been trying to walk to the roadway on its western side. But, just as she began to get their bearings, she saw thick night clouds gathering like great fists, rising up to beat out the blaze of the sunset.

Kerrie stamped her feet against the hardening ground and wished she could find a way to dam back the dark.

Skip was falling behind again. Kerrie waited for him. He hadn't spoken since his outburst over the children, hours ago now. Their last hope, for a moon, seemed unlikely in that solid sky.

'Rest,' Skip croaked.

'No, keep walking,' Kerrie ordered.

'I canny. I'll just die on my feet instead of lying down.' Skip sank to the ground and groaned. 'Aah, soft. 'S'like a bed.'

Kerrie flopped beside him on the spongy heather. Oh, to just curl up and sleep, too exhausted to feel.

She dragged herself back and shoved Skip onwards. If they gave themselves targets it might be easier. Make it to the next ridge and then rest.

Skip was sprawled in the heather before they'd quite made it, but it was near enough. Already the dark had closed in. Kerrie found a rock to sit on, fearful of the comfort of the heather. The flat plateau with its litter of odd-shaped rocks reminded her uncannily of the roof-top. Another mind-trick. If she could only find a single light, even a star, in all that dark.

Kerrie felt the thud of her heart as something split the blackness in front of her. What was it? A snail's trail of silver with a crack of moon at the end of it? A track leading up to the sky?

No, she saw it now. It was moonlight shining on the railway track.

There was only the sound of their footsteps. Even the sliver of moon was gulped back into the dark. But the railway track felt solid and safe under their feet after the shifting rocks and sucking peat-bogs of the moor.

'Listen,' said Skip. They stopped. The metal of the railway track still had the echo of a ring in it from the vibration of their steps.

'If we walked till we were out of the world there

wouldny even be a pile of stones to say we'd been here. We'd fade like a tune in the air.'

'Shut up, Skip. Keep a grip. We're walking to the next stop.'

'Could be miles away. We need a rest, food. Go on when it's light.'

'Food? Give me a clue,' groaned Kerrie.

'Roots,' Skip answered.

'Roots?'

'Aye, tree roots. My book said the cattle reivers who lived on the moor in olden times ate them. Stopped them starving.'

All of a sudden he skidded down the stone-chip siding of the railway track. Kerrie couldn't be bothered. She sat and heard digging, soft thuds and splashing. Skip scrambled back up the embankment.

'Roots,' he announced, and thrust a bundle of wet twigs at her.

'I don't fancy being poisoned,' said Kerrie.

'Oh, you prefer the slow starvation.' Skip chewed on a root, spat then swallowed. 'The bark's bitter. Peel that and it's no' awful bad. It's that or grass.'

Kerrie peeled and chewed. It was sharp and tangy, not inedible. She had gone past the hunger mark anyway. She looked into the dark.

'Something.' The words caught in her throat with the stringy root. 'There's something over there.'

Skip stood up.

'Those kids. Right then.'

'No, look, a house. It's got a wee chimney, see?'

168

The moon obligingly made a tear in the thick sky and they could see clearer. A hut sat at the side of the railway track. Its walls seemed wrinkled. Skip clanged down the railway line and chapped them.

'Metal walls. What's it for?' he wondered.

'The railway workers, I suppose,' said Kerrie.

'If it's good enough for them . . .' said Skip. He began to kick in the rusted door. It was like breaking open a pine cone, only this was the concentrated smell of old cupboards, hoarding years of undisturbed dust.

'I think I've lived this bit before,' said Kerrie. 'I suppose those kids got your matches.'

'Luckily they're in my secret compartment' Skip fumbled in the lining of his coat. 'Wish I'd put the rest of my stuff in there.'

The match flickered, casting up a tiny room littered with crumpled newspaper, coal sacks and tin cans. There was a fire-grate against one wall. Skip was immediately at work, stuffing paper into the grate and lighting it, kicking cans aside and spreading sacks on the floor. The hut filled with choking smoke and Kerrie retreated for air. She heard banging, then there was a belch of sparking ash and smoke from the tiny chimney.

After a while Skip emerged in a fit of coughing. 'Give it a wee while to calm down. You still got those roots?'

Kerrie took them from her pocket. 'Don't burn the place down.'

'It's all metal, even the roof. Weird.' Skip was

suddenly all businesslike. 'Right – you go and find some more roots and I'll roast these.'

'Yum.'

Kerrie returned with torn hands to find the smoke had died down. Instead the hut was full of a spicy aroma and a small pile of charred roots lay beside a couple of rusted tin cans.

'You'll make somebody a wonderful husband. I'm no' drinking out of that though.'

'I cleaned them,' Skip protested.

They chewed and the rain began to ring on the roof.

'Chicken curry,' said Skip. 'You can kid yourself. You can.'

'Tough chicken,' said Kerrie.

'A drop of wine, madam?'

'Hate the stuff.'

'Pure mountain water with a dash of peat.'

'In ye olde rustic goblet,' giggled Kerrie, holding up her tin can.

'You're getting the hang of it,' nodded Skip.

They chewed, watching the fire eat up newspaper.

'Avalon,' said Kerrie. 'You never told me what it was.'

'Ach, a con by the looks of things. It was in one of my stories. These Celtic tribes lived on the moor in olden times – it was all a forest then, all this – and they wandered their whole lives looking for some place called Avalon. They thought it was like heaven on earth. Divine Avalon. But I think your gran was maybe right about that. And it said gypsies and restless souls today probably had Celtic ancestors.'

'What?' Kerrie sat up.

'Maybe that's what we had,' said Skip. 'Maybe we'll wander forever.'

Kerrie stared at him. 'My dad wandered off. Then my mum started. Now it's me. It's like a family disease.'

'Weird,' said Skip. He sounded interested but he didn't probe further.

'And the Restless Souls – that was the name of our band. Shell thought it up. Her mum always called us that.'

'Super weird,' said Skip.

The wind cast up waves on the moor, battering them off the sides of the metal hut.

'I used to imagine he'd come back for me,' said Kerrie.

'Your dad? Why? Was he good to you?' Skip asked.

Kerrie thought. 'I don't remember.' She took a chance. 'You've never said anything about your folks. Tell me about them.'

Wind blew smoke back down the chimney, rain hammered like nails on the walls. Kerrie clasped her knees and chewed her fingers. He could sit glowering all night now. But he just shook his head.

'Something happened to my dad.' Skip spoke warily. He looked around him as if worried that someone was lurking, listening, in the dark corners of the tiny hut. 'It was like he died. He gave up on everything. Everyone. Himself. And he just took it out on us.'

'What happened?'

'Don't know.'

'You said us,' said Kerrie. 'Your mum?'

'Uh-uh.'

'Where's she now?'

Skip crushed the last bits of newspaper and threw them on the fire.

'Don't know. Still with him maybe, dead maybe.'

'You sound like you hate her,' said Kerrie. 'But if it was him . . .'

'Aye, but she stayed, she wouldny leave him. She'd rather her kid froze on the streets, anything, than do us both a favour and leave him to it. You canny change someone else. But she thought she could.'

'She might be frantic about you,' said Kerrie.

'Well. You're one to talk. Anyway, she chose him, didn't she?'

They sat unspeaking as a battle broke out on the moor. Rain came down the chimney and the fire spluttered. Mrs McCormack had begun, softly at first but louder and louder now that Kerrie was ignoring her, to rap with her knuckles on the metal walls of the hut, just like she used to rap on Shell's bedroom door when the music got too loud or Shell kept up a prolonged drum practice on her upturned wastepaper bin. Mrs McCormack was demanding that Kerrie hear her out. 'Your mum's all washed up,' she was shouting over the noise of the wind. 'It's a shame, Kerrie, a right shame. What would your gran say?'

'In the morning we'll just follow the track,' said Skip eventually, breaking through the din. 'You canny get lost on a railway line. Run over by a train maybe. Be

172

just our luck.' He looked up. 'Is that your teeth chittering? Take deep breaths, don't shiver against it. We'll use my coat as a blanket.'

His breath was warm on her nose.

'I wish you'd been around last winter on the roof,' he said. 'I nearly froze to death some nights. Ice in my body and my head. It'd come down on me like a cage. I made up a safe wee world in my head but sometimes I thought, I'll never get back out.

'It's no' our mess,' said Skip, as Kerrie didn't answer. She was busy fighting off Mrs McCormack in her head. 'Forget them. You should see the red suns over the city in the winter. The worst cold you can imagine and the most brilliant thing I've ever seen. I wonder what it's like out here. Red suns on a sea of snow. You'd think you were on the moon.'

'This is our own mess,' said Kerrie. 'Well and truly.'

Skip sighed warmth over her face. Kerrie took a deep breath.

'If we went back we'd maybe lose each other. And we'd lose our music.'

'Sounds like too much to lose,' said Skip. He yawned again, deeply, and Kerrie felt a burst of warm air against her freezing ear. She should have kept her long hair after all, she thought. Sunk in his instant sleep, Skip was already oblivious to the cold. And to Mrs McCormack's unstoppable monologue from outside the hut door.

Kerrie woke with the sound of Skip's mouth organ in her head. She opened the hut door. The storm still moaned around, mingling now with the wail of the mouth organ. Kerrie pressed the sharp edge of the hut wall into her hand, felt it, and the music went on. She could see nothing.

Skip muttered in his sleep.

Am I dreaming? Kerrie wondered, staring out at the sound of the mouth organ hidden somewhere in the dark.

She began to walk towards the sound. A luminosity hung in the dark in front of her. As she lipped a rise in the land, Kerrie saw the children gathered round a fire in the circle of boulders that sat in a dip of the moor. The oldest girl was holding the sparkly so that it caught the light of the flames, and the other children sat entranced as its lights shot high into the dark. She spun round and round, her feet moving in time to the jig the boy now played, and the tiniest child laughed and tried to catch the sparks that whirled from it.

'Kerrie! Where are you?'

It was Skip, somewhere back in the dark. He sounded terrified.

'Over here,' she called. 'I've found them. Look.'

The music cut dead. They must have heard her. She should have kept quiet. Kerrie saw the children disappear behind the boulders. Then out of the dark came the thump of something moving over the land.

'Kerrie,' called Skip, somewhere close behind. 'Kerrie, come back.'

Out of the black came points of fire. They moved downwards through the black and grew to flames. The slow thump of hoofs deepened and there were shouts. The girl was stamping out the fire among the boulders, sparks catching at her clothes. She disappeared again as the horses came over the ridge.

Kerrie looked up into the face of a man that was vicious in the light of his torch flame.

The man saw the fire embers and grinned.

'Are they real? Are they?' Kerrie called out. But she had lost Skip.

The riders were circling the boulders.

'Out wi' ye or ye'll burn. We'll burn ye out like the rats ye are,' shouted one.

The first flame hit the grass and, as it struggled to feed, the children scattered from the boulders. There was a confusion of fire, shouts as the riders swathed the dark with their torches.

'I'll have your burnt head for the king, lass! He'll reward me for it.'

A scream tore the dark apart and there came a burst of fire. There was wind on Kerrie's face as a horse reared and charged. 'They couldn't,' she gasped. No one could do this to another human being, to a child. It wasn't possible.

It must all be in her head, she told herself. They had imagined the moor children all along and she could stop it all if she concentrated hard and broke through the dream. She must find Skip, tell him. She began to turn back, then saw one of the riders had gripped the oldest girl by the arm. He swung from his saddle and flung her to the ground.

'Kerrie, get back to the hut,' she heard Skip shout, far away now, frantic. 'I'm going back. Kerrie!'

But Kerrie was sliding down the grass. At the foot of the slope all she could see was fire and red smoke. Her face blazed with it. Then Kerrie saw the girl scramble across the ground in front of her, struggling to rip herself from the man's grasp. He used his torch to back her against a boulder.

'Swear tae your king or you'll burn first, MacGregor scum. A beheading's kinder.'

The girl turned her face to the rock as the man grabbed a strand of her hair and set it alight.

Kerrie scrabbled for wood or stone. There was nothing. She saw a glint in the grass, felt the sharp slice of frozen metal. She aimed it at the level of the man's face.

His expression stalled her and she glanced up at her own hand. She held the sparkly. It took the blaze of the torch and shot it back at the man in lasers of coloured light. He backed away, and as Kerrie tracked him he screamed to the other riders.

Kerrie twisted the sparkly and sprays of coloured laser spiked the dark. Beside her, the girl had beaten out the fire with her hands.

'Hold on to me. Follow me,' Kerrie ordered.

They moved together and beat back the riders.

'It's witchery!'

'Devilry!'

'MacGregor evil!'

A torch burned in the air above her head and Kerrie

dived aside. It splintered on a rock. She took a chance and ran for the riders, holding the sparkly high.

'It's witchery all right and if it catches you it'll split you into a million pieces!'

There was panic, shouts, hoofs reared and in moments the hillside was clear.

Kerrie turned.

She was alone in the thick, closed dark of the moor.

There was nothing but the dark. No light in the sky, no mountain shadow or line of hill that she could follow. Even the storm had gone now leaving Kerrie alone in the silent, hardening cold. Bars began to close around her, tight against her chest. Kerrie curled up into a ball in the stiff heather, made an enclosure with her arms, and breathed her own warmth on to her hands and face.

Skip's ice-cage had found her and if she slept it might keep her inside for good.

Hard sunlight on her face woke her up. When Kerrie tried to move she found the cage of ice had frozen her to the ground. She forced movement, limb by limb, and sat up.

The moor sparkled, white and innocent in the morning sun. A crescent moon and a few stars hung in a fairytale sky. The star straight above her winked red and purple. She saw the whole night in one thought and closed her eyes.

'Found you.'

Kerrie opened her eyes. Skip's head blocked out the star. His face was as white as the frost.

'You OK?' he said, his voice a thin wheeze.

Kerrie shook her head. He sounded strange, as if he'd swallowed his mouth organ, blowing through it on every breath.

'Thought I'd never find you,' he said. 'Here, you left your guitar in the hut.' He unstrapped it from his back and collapsed on the ground, coughing up a cloud of white vapour. At last he stopped and rubbed his chest, gasping breaths of icy air.

'You're ill,' she said.

'Uh-uh.'

He wheezed a few coughs and restrained a full-blown fit.

Kerrie stood up and hugged her arms round herself, following the long, glistening trail of the railway line with her eyes.

'There's no' been a single train,' said Skip. 'Maybe it's an old line. I'd never make it anyway. You go on.'

She just tutted.

'The frost's starting to melt,' she said. 'Was it all a dream?'

Skip coughed, his head down. 'What?'

'Last night,' said Kerrie, watching him closely. 'The children, the men on horses – was it real?'

She stopped. He wasn't listening, or didn't want to talk about it. He was staring up at the mountain in front of them.

'It's amazing what your mind does to you when it's stressed out,' he wheezed. 'I've been there before.'

Kerrie followed Skip's stare. There was a faint grating noise between his wheezes.

'Is that just a buzzing in my head or do you hear something?' he asked. 'I'm a bit flaky.'

'It's maybe the slow starvation starting.'

'Aye.'

A dark spot appeared in the sky above the mountains. The noise sharpened and now they could see it was a helicopter. It circled the moor ponderously.

Kerrie looked at herself and Skip, both stained the colours of the moor.

'They'll never see us in all this. It's evil, this place.'

Skip was trying to light the cold ground with his matches.

'Go and stand on a white patch.' He tossed the matchbox. 'It's only a place,' he said. 'It's people that are bad. Make evil things happen.'

The helicopter seemed undecided. The sun glinted on it as it began to turn away.

'Oh God.'

'Who's he?' muttered Skip.

A reflected sunbeam flashed from the helicopter.

The sparkly, thought Kerrie. Of course. How on earth could she have forgotten that? She must have it about her somewhere. That and the green paper jewel in the corner of her pocket were all she'd had to hold on to in all that dark. She'd clung to them like rocks in a stormy sea and wished for a bit of moon or starlight, but the sparkly had lain dead in her hands as if its energy had run its course.

Kerrie fished about her pockets and found it.

She held it high to the sun.

'My sparkly, you found my sparkly!' Skip exploded into another fit beside her as the sparkly burst into light.

Jumping the gap

The helicopter nosed back round towards the mountains. In a moment it would be gone. Kerrie flashed sunlight in the sparkly over and over but it was no use. Then, just as they'd expected it to disappear over the shoulder of the mountain, the helicopter seemed to change its mind. It dithered, nosing this way and that. In a spurt of decisiveness the helicopter swung round again to face them. It swooped down, down until it was directly over the hollow. Wind blasted in their faces, tearing at their clothes and flattening the moor grasses as the helicopter parked beside the circle of boulders.

Mauve ran over the melting frost and slithered to a stop a few steps away from Kerrie.

'I'm sorry,' she said. She looked nervous. 'I told on you. I didny know what to do when the storm came. It nearly blew the caravan over. You said you'd phone the farmhouse if you were in trouble and I kept thinking they'd phone, surely, and let me know if they're safe.'

'I wondered if she'd remember us. She's such a dope

181

when she's stuck in a painting,' said Skip. He grabbed Mauve, hugged her and collapsed coughing.

Kerrie grinned. 'He's half dead,' she explained. 'You're a hero, Mauve. We thought we were goners.'

Mauve looked relieved.

Skip saluted the men who had sprung from the helicopter with blankets and a medical bag.

'I think I need a wee hand here, guys,' he wheezed. His rescuers looked unimpressed.

'I'm glad to find you so chirpy, sonny. I'm surprised we found you at all,' said one. He flung a blanket round Skip's shoulders and helped him towards the helicopter.

'That's just why we're so chirpy,' Skip told him. 'We're hysterical with relief.'

Skip stopped dead. He kneeled in the grass and picked up a couple of blackened objects.

'My book! My moothie!'

The mouth organ was bashed and discoloured as if it had lain under a rock in a peat-bog for a couple of hundred years. The book was peat-coated and wrinkled. But Skip didn't care. He hugged them to himself under his coat and got into the helicopter.

From the air, they saw the moor stretch out like a sea.

We'd never have made it, thought Kerrie, her eye following the silver stretch of railway line far into the distance.

'A draw,' wheezed Skip. 'We never got ourselves back, but the monster moor didny beat us.'

He frowned and Kerrie hesitated; she'd better own up to Skip about what she'd just done with his sparkly.

They were given mugfuls of hot tea. Below, the moor was beginning to steam gently like a pot off the boil.

Kerrie sipped her tea. The episode with the moor children seemed so unlikely now that they were back in the real world again. Maybe we just imagined it all up in a hypothermic trance, she thought. Or maybe I did.

The helicopter lurched into a turn. She'd have to tell him.

'Skip,' she whispered. 'I left the sparkly for them. Special protection.' At the last moment, some impulse had made Kerrie run back to leave the sparkly lying in the grass beside one of the boulders.

'I saw,' he wheezed.

'I'll get you a new one, I promise.'

'Aye, well. It was just a toy. A useless thing,' he tried to grin. 'I was outgrowing it anyway.'

Kerrie grabbed his hand.

Skip frowned and hunched inside his blanket. He shuddered a few coughs.

The helicopter dipped towards the ground and Kerrie saw a patch of black tarmac looming. In one corner of the black, positioned like a couple of postage stamps, were the small, white, rectangular shapes of an ambulance and a police car.

'The sound's all over the place. Out of control. Totally.'

Skip sat hunched up in the hospital bed polishing his dented and blackened mouth organ with a bit of blanket. He looked most unlike himself with a scrubbed-clean face and horrendous green stripy pyjamas that were too short in the arms for him. He had tried to disguise the fact that his hair was as clean as his face, and had been in contact with a comb, by scrabbling it up into its usual mess. But its newly washed state made him look as if he'd just stuck a finger in a live socket.

He was awful twitchy. It wasn't just the pyjamas or the mouth organ that was bothering him, thought Kerrie. There was something else. She wondered if he'd had news of his mum yet. Maybe that was it.

Skip put the warped mouth organ to his lips and let Kerrie hear the caterwauling. A nurse sent a steely glance from the other side of the ward.

'I'm no' exactly collecting a fan club either.'

'Try it again, softer,' Kerrie suggested.

Angela the social worker coughed gently from a seat at the end of Skip's bed. They both ignored her.

'On you go.'

Skip let out a gentler wail. His frown loosened as he tried his haunting rooftop melody. The notes distorted, twisted and whorled around the tune.

The nurse marched over.

Kerrie stared at Skip's bottle of Tizer.

Angela stood up and made a fuss about gathering up her coat and bag, dropping one after the other in the process.

'It's in there,' said Kerrie.

'I've told you I don't want to hear that racket again,'

the nurse snapped, glancing over a sheet clipped to the end of Skip's bed. 'When was your last check-up?'

'Nearly time to go, Kerrie,' murmured Angela.

'What's in there?' Skip demanded.

'The sparkly. That's the sound of it. Skip,' Kerrie hesitated. 'I keep wondering if we went back to the moor one night maybe we'd see something, maybe they'd be playing with the sparkly. Then we'd know for sure if it was all real.'

'Um.'

Skip frowned at Angela and the nurse who were muttering together at the foot of his bed. Kerrie played with a frayed bit on her jacket. Every time she tried to talk about the moor, tried to gauge what he remembered or thought, it was the same. He avoided the question, sank into a mood, and made her feel stupid.

'You'll remember and write to Mauve, won't you? Care of Brae Farm.' They didn't have much time left and Kerrie would rather babble than let her last minutes with Skip end in one of his sullen silences.

'I know, I know,' said Skip. He coughed loudly. 'Could we have five minutes in private?' he suddenly demanded of the two women at the foot of his bed. 'Just a tiny, wee, basic human right. She'll no kidnap me. No' in these pyjamas, anyway.'

Skip employed his most impressive glare. After a bit of hesitation Angela and the nurse retreated.

'What's up?' asked Kerrie.

Skip was feeling about under his pillow. He brought out his book. His hands were trembling.

'There's something in here,' he said. He opened the book at a page with a turned-down corner and stared at it.

'I've read it over and over since I found it. I don't know what I think. Listen. It happened in sixteen something or other. The MacGregors were cattle reivers and they lived on the moor as bandits, it says. They were the only ones who knew all the paths across it – they had it tamed all right.' He was gabbling, tripping over words. 'See, the Campbells were after MacGregor land. They had a feud going with them, and they got the king to order the whole MacGregor clan to death – sounds like he was fed up with the lot of them and the MacGregors got it 'cause they were causing havoc on the moor.'

'What happened?' Kerrie asked.

'The MacGregors got wiped out. And the Campbells got the land they'd been after. But a band of the MacGregor children escaped. They hid out on the moor, outcasts from the rest of the world.' He met Kerrie's eyes, then he huffed a laugh. 'Aye, they survived too. They'd mug passing travellers for whatever they could get.'

'You don't say.' Kerrie grinned at the thought of the tiny tot with the stick.

Skip grimaced. He traced a couple of lines in his book with his finger. 'It says other outlaws could get pardons from the king if they brought him a MacGregor's head.'

'What, even a kiddie?'

Skip nodded. 'Sick, eh? So gangs went out searching the moor for them.'

Kerrie felt her stomach turn.

'And then,' he said, 'it gives this story about a witch. She steps out of flames in a ring of stones when the children are attacked one night. She saves them.'

Skip found the place and began to read.

' "Spears of many-coloured light burst from the witch's fingers and struck the outlaws, burning out men's eyes, hurling them back into the dark, and they fled in terror. To this day, shepherds will steer their flocks clear of the circle of stones in the hollow of the moor. They tell of a strange corona of light that hangs there and of children's laughter. Even in daylight it is an unearthly place, shrouded in mists. Who knows but the MacGregor children and their kindly witch still play there, whirling up enchantments and curses on their enemies." '

Skip shut the book with a thump. An old man at the far side of the ward called plaintively for a bedpan. Kerrie picked the book from the bedclothes as if it might burst into flame at her touch.

'A hundred and sixteen,' said Skip. 'It'll still be there. I've checked loads of times.'

Kerrie located the passage and read it, several times. She couldn't get her mind around it. It was too big a thought. To jump the gap of three centuries like a spark of electricity bridging the space between electrodes, linking them. To exist for a single burning moment in history, as a witch. Had she really changed what would have been? The terrible thing that would have been.

Kerrie touched the words on the page. Unbelievable; yet there it was. She felt Skip's dark eyes watch her and cupped her hands over her face.

'Are you telling me you saw it after all? Did you? Tell me what you remember,' Kerrie demanded.

'I canny remember anything much of the whole thing,' Skip said at last. 'Just the fog and the moor going on and on then all that dark. I remember we found the hut, then later I lost you in the dark. I heard something coming, the deer or something else, and I was scared, I just ran. I kept running and falling, and then I don't know. I was stuck in the dark, scared out my mind. I know there's something else, but it's sitting away at the back of my head. I canny reach it.'

'This.' Kerrie pointed to the book. 'This is what I think I remember.'

'Uh-uh.' Skip nodded. He sat thinking. 'I believe it's possible,' he said. 'If you believe in things hard enough you can make them happen. I showed you before with the sparkly, didn't I?'

The nurse gave them a time's-up look on her return journey with the bedpan.

Kerrie began to panic. They needed more time.

'When do we get to see each other again? Nobody'll give me an answer.'

'It depends,' said Angela, suddenly at her side again.

188

Angela was a pain, like a stray dog always trotting at your heel. Kerrie felt she'd hardly been out of the woman's sight since the other day when she had arrived back in the city in the police car. Skip had been ferried by ambulance.

It had seemed a long lifetime since Kerrie had seen so many people and buildings. The noise and movement of it all had flattened her to the back seat of the police car. The lazy tick-tick-tick of the car indicator at the traffic lights, the crush of schoolchildren on a passing bus, the sun blinding like fire on steel on the wet road between the cars – everything was exactly the same as before yet so strange, as if the world had tilted on its axis, subtly shifting the angle of things.

After hours at the police station, Kerrie had been taken to a foster home where she was made welcome by a kind, easy-going couple who didn't crowd in on her and ran her a bath and left her to soak for as long as she wanted in the peace of their pink and blue bathroom.

Next morning, in the middle of a long, tearful phone call to Shell, Angela had arrived with a letter from Mum. There were hard dots here and there in the margins where Kerrie saw Mum had stopped, stuck for words, her pen tapping out its own frantic SOS.

Something in Mum's letter, something about the way she didn't plead or promise the world, just asked for another chance, struck at Kerrie's heart. Phil was gone, Mum said. And good riddance, she'd scribbled in the margin, with three exclamation marks.

Kerrie ran upstairs and fished out Gran's letter from deep inside the lining of her guitar cover where she had kept it, unread, all this time. She had stuffed it away there, knowing she couldn't tear it up, no matter how angry and upset she was with Gran.

But now she was ready to read it. She needed Gran's help.

Kerrie locked herself in the pink and blue bathroom and took the letter from its badly crumpled envelope.

She stared at the page, imagining Gran at the kitchen table, furrowing her hair into a mess as she wrote.

The letter was to the point, as Gran always was. *Be strong, Kerrie,* she had written. *Your mum broke the chain and she's suffered for it. Maybe you can start to mend it. But it wasn't all her fault, remember. Your dad walked out on you both. The two of you are all that's left so you have to try. I've told her the same. And don't bother yourself about me. I expect I'll bump into your grandpa.*

Daft old woman, thought Kerrie. There must have been a letter for Mum too, then.

It was the only time, Kerrie realized, Gran had ever mentioned Dad since his disappearance. And she blamed him. For the first time Kerrie saw how angry Gran must have been with Dad, so angry it had kept her from speaking about him.

Yet all this time Kerrie had seen Dad as a romantic, driven soul, swept out into the world by his passion to explore. She had blamed Mum for Dad leaving, had held her responsible for letting him go. The fact was, as

190

Gran pointed out, Dad had abandoned them and he never looked back.

You canny change someone else. Skip had said that. Mum couldn't have made Dad stay. Just as when Kerrie ran away to the rooftop and then up north, no one – neither Mum nor Shell – had the power to make her stay.

So Dad had left. Mum had gone to pieces. And Kerrie had turned her back on it all for a new life with Gran. A chain of events leaving a broken chain. And now, perhaps, mended by the last link in the chain. Herself.

But could she mend it? Kerrie wondered. Rescuing the MacGregor children and beating the moor might in the end prove a lesser challenge than jumping the gap between her and Mum.

Kerrie had quickly told Skip about the letters, Mum's and Gran's.

'What will I do?' she asked him.

'What does your stomach tell you?' he said. 'You should go by that.'

'My stomach's in knots,' Kerrie had answered. Perhaps it would work, she thought, at least for a year until she and Skip could, literally, get their act together. She'd be sixteen then, old enough to take control of her own life.

Angela had butted in with her support.

'I'm not asking you to like me, Kerrie,' she'd said. 'But use me, let me be piggy-in-the-middle between you and your mum. Shove some of the hassle on to me – it's what I get paid for, after all.'

'Kerrie, we have to get going, pet. There's your mum to see today, remember.' Angela began rustling about in her bag. She was doing her softly-softly act.

'Where'll you be?' Kerrie asked Skip. He had his own social worker.

Skip blew out a 'who knows?' sigh. 'My mum's coming to see me this afternoon,' he said. He polished away at the mouth-organ, frowning over a scratch on the metal. 'I've written to Doo. I need to tell him everything. Wish I could live with him,' he finished wistfully.

'Listen,' said Kerrie. 'Saturdays, the shopping precinct. Whenever we can make it.'

'Nice knowing you, Kerrie.' He did his disinterested act but his hand was damp as she squeezed it.

Typical, she thought. Ten steps forward, nine steps back. Skip still needed a lot of mending inside. Skip, Mauve, the moor children, Mum, herself: Kerrie thought of all the mending needed.

There had been enough suffering all round, she decided.

Somewhere in her pocket was the tiny parcel of Gran's green sweet paper. She felt around and found it.

'I was thinking if we can change the past, maybe we can do something with the future. You never know,' she said. 'It was you that saved those kids as much as me. I couldny have done it without your sparkly, now could I?'

Kerrie pressed the shiny, green, sweet paper into

Skip's hand. He looked at it, then at her, with wide, soft brown eyes.

Kerrie found she had to look away. She stood up and walked over to the window at the head of Skip's bed. She stared out, gathering up the courage she needed to leave.

The hospital crested a hill and from the window Kerrie could look out over the jumbled spread of the city to the cluster of tower blocks raised high on their own hump of hill. Far beyond them, soft purple smudges on the skyline, the land rose into mountains.

There was a sudden spark of something away to the left. Kerrie shaded her eyes against the low winter sun and saw it was the dockyard cranes glinting beside a stretch of sun-specked river. The cranes looked so small and spindly, she thought. Just feeble fingers reaching up to a sky as vast and wide open as a deep blue ocean.

And now she really had to go. And Skip was left alone with it all whirling in his head, just as she was. But he would manage, Kerrie felt sure. He had his mouth organ and the music and his book. And he had her promise, her tiny, green, paper jewel, pressed in the palm of his hand.

Also available now from Young Picador

JULIE BERTAGNA

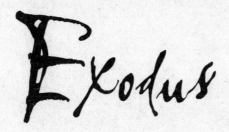

The world is gradually drowning. As mighty Arctic icecaps melt, the seas rise and land disappears for-ever beneath storm-tossed waves. Mara's island community has no choice – they must leave their homes and set sail in the ultimate exodus. Packed into tiny boats, they begin a terrifying journey to an extraordinary city that rises from the sea. But they are shunned, not allowed to enter this New World. The outcome for the unwanted refugees can only be disastrous.

Mara is desperate to survive – but her quest will become something even greater – a journey into humanity's capacity for good and evil. And a heart-wrenching story of love and loss . . .

JULIE BERTAGNA

the opposite of chocolate

It's a long, hot summer – and a climactic one. For fourteen-year-old Sapphire it brings the awesome, terrifying realization that she is pregnant – a discovery that catapults her into the eye of a storm as her body, her future, her life, become a battleground for everyone's needs but her own. Meanwhile, out in the humid urban night, a mysterious firebug is running wild, working out his own anger and confusion with dramatic consequences. Somehow, from this cauldron of emotion and fear, Sapphire must find a way to take control of her life – and make the most agonizing and lonely of choices.

Julie Bertagna

Soundtrack

Finn Silverweed lives in the fishing village of Laggandall Bay. He feels like a complete outsider: he doesn't want to be part of the close-knit community of fishermen, but nor can he stand the idea of following his dad and working at the nearby naval base. So Finn spends his time trying to block out the world – through listening to music and by rowing out to his secret cove.

But Finn can't escape the strange things that are happening – and he's scared. A comet looms like an omen over the bay, and Finn is haunted by weird noises in his head that draw him to the sea. Disaster threatens – and no one in Laggandall will escape untouched . . .

A selected list of titles
available from Young Picador

The prices shown below are correct at the time of going to press. However, Macmillan Publishers reserves the right to show new retail prices on covers which may differ from those previously advertised.

JULIE BERTAGNA

Exodus	0 330 39908 X	£5.99
The Opposite of Chocolate	0 330 39746 X	£4.99
Soundtrack	0 330 41813 0	£4.99

All Pan Macmillan titles can be ordered from our website, www.panmacmillan.com, or from your local bookshop and are also available by post from:

**Bookpost,
PO Box 29, Douglas, Isle of Man IM99 1BQ**

Credit cards accepted. For details:
Telephone: 01624 677237
Fax: 01624 670923
Email: bookshop@enterprise.net
www.bookpost.co.uk

Free postage and packing in the United Kingdom